The Snowman

One by one, the store lights went out. Each store seemed to darken as she passed. She had the eerie feeling that she was causing them to go out.

Her sneakers slid on the slushy snow. She tried to remember why she had parked so far from the restaurant.

This area of the parking lot was nearly deserted.

It was eerily quiet. She had never liked the parking lot after the mall had closed. It was too large, too dark, too empty. It made her feel so vulnerable.

She stopped when she heard the footsteps behind her. Soft footsteps in the fresh, wet snow.

Fast.

Faster.

Coming toward her.

Also in the
Point Horror Series:

Look out for:

THE SNOWMAN

Point Horror

R. L. Stine

Hippo Books
Scholastic Children's Books
London

Scholastic Children's Books,
Scholastic Publications Ltd,
7-9 Pratt Street, London NW1 0AE, UK

Scholastic Inc.,
730 Broadway, New York, NY 10003, USA

Scholastic Canada Ltd,
123 Newkirk Road, Richmond Hill,
Ontario, Canada L4C 3G5

Ashton Scholastic Pty Ltd,
P O Box 579, Gosford, New South Wales,
Australia

Ashton Scholastic Ltd,
Private Bag 1, Penrose, Auckland,
New Zealand

First published in the USA by Scholastic Inc., 1991
First published in the UK by Scholastic Publications Ltd, 1992

Copyright © R. L. Stine, 1991

ISBN 0 590 55065 9

Printed by Cox & Wyman Ltd, Reading, Berks

THE SNOWMAN

Chapter 1

"Uncle James, where are you?"

"I'm up here, Heather. Up here on the roof."

Heather zipped her down jacket up to the collar and trudged around the corner of the house, her boots crunching on the ice-hard snow.

"Up here, Heather."

"I see you," Heather called, shielding her eyes with one mittened hand as she peered up at her uncle on the snow-covered roof. Long, pointed icicles hung in a row from the gutter, dripping onto the snow below.

"Hold the ladder for me, will you? I patched up the leak. Now I'm coming down," Uncle James said, his face red from the cold. On his hands and knees, in his ancient olive-colored overcoat, with his long, bony arms and legs, he looked like some kind of gigantic insect.

Heather slipped, lost her footing, and fell onto her knees.

"Hurry up, will you?" he snapped, impatient as always.

"I'm coming. I'm coming," Heather muttered, picking herself up slowly, brushing the snow off the knees of her jeans.

"I'm freezing to death up here," Uncle James complained. "Why are you always in slow motion?"

Heather gripped the sides of the aluminum ladder. A strong gust of wind nearly blew her and the ladder over. She leaned forward against the wind, repositioning herself to get a better grip.

"Hold it steady!" Uncle James screamed. "I told you — I'm freezing to death!"

"What a good idea," Heather said, watching her uncle on his hands and knees, struggling to back over the snow-filled gutter onto the ladder.

"What did you say?"

Heather didn't reply. She wrapped her mittened hands tightly around the sides of the metal ladder.

"I heard that," her uncle shouted. Only his boots and the back of his coat were visible to her. "You will be grounded for that remark, Heather."

"It wasn't a remark. I *meant* it," Heather said, peering up at him into the silver afternoon sunlight.

As he cautiously lowered one boot onto the top rung of the ladder, she pulled with all her strength.

The ladder tilted away from the house. Heather let go and moved quickly out of the way. The ladder fell onto the snow with a loud *crunch*.

"Hey!"

Her uncle scrambled back up onto the roof, his black-gloved hands scrabbling frantically over the snow-covered shingles. He looks like a big, green squirrel, Heather thought, chuckling to herself.

"Hey! Are you crazy?" he screamed, sitting down on the snow, turning to face her, his face red with fury. He swore at her and called her his usual string of ugly names. "Put that ladder back up!"

" 'Bye, Uncle," Heather called calmly. She gave him a little wave with her red-mittened hand and started to walk down the driveway to the street.

"Get back here! Where are you going?"

She kept walking. She didn't look back.

"Put that ladder back — now!" Another string of abusive names.

You have such a foul mouth, Uncle James, Heather thought, turning right at the street and heading up the hill. Maybe you will freeze with your mouth wide open. I'd like to see that.

"I'll freeze to death up here!" he shouted, his voice muffled now by the snow-laden trees.

"That's the idea!" Heather called without turning back.

Chapter 2

No, no. That's all wrong, Heather thought.

That's not good enough. Much too slow.

She closed her eyes and pictured her uncle up on the snow-covered roof again. "Heather, hold the ladder," he called. "I'm coming down now."

"I've got it," she shouted up to him, gripping the ladder on both sides. The metal felt cold right through her mittens. She adjusted her feet. The snow was deep and hard. A layer of ice had formed like a crust over the surface.

"Hold it steady," Uncle James ordered, placing one boot, then the other on the top rung.

Heather waited until he had descended a bit, his boots on the third rung, his long, bony hands gripping the top rung above his head.

Then she pulled with all her strength.

Yes!

The ladder swung quickly away from the house.

Heather let go and stepped back to watch.

"Hey — !"

Behind his thick eyeglasses, Uncle James's eyes opened wide with fright and surprise.

The ladder was standing straight up now, supported by nothing, about to come crashing down onto the snow.

"Close your mouth, Uncle James. You'll drop your teeth!" Heather enjoyed the terrified look on his face, the way he gripped the top rung so tightly, even though the ladder was about to carry him down to his death.

And then the ladder toppled over onto the snow.

The loud *crunch*, the sound of an egg cracking — that was Uncle James.

What a nasty fall, Heather thought. Her laughter echoed off the heavy, white trees.

"What are you thinking about, Heather?" Ben asked, pulling away from her.

She could still taste his lips on hers. "Oh. Sorry," she said, her fantasy still lingering in her mind.

She shook her head as if trying to shake away her thoughts. Okay. Now I'm back, she thought. I'm sitting in the front seat of Ben's Honda Civic. And I was kissing him.

"You seemed a million miles away," Ben said, removing his arm from around her shoulder. He raked his hand back through his straight black hair and stared at her questioningly with his large, dark eyes. "You were thinking about dinner, right? You were fantasizing that I was a giant roast beef."

"Yuck," Heather said, giving him a playful shove on the shoulder. Ben was a good guy. He could always make her laugh. "Nope. You were a turkey."

"Hey, that's what everyone calls me!" he joked.

Her expression turned solemn. "No, I was thinking about Uncle James."

"Oh, that's *real* flattering," Ben said, gripping the steering wheel with both hands, rolling his eyes, acting offended. "You're kissing me and you're thinking about your uncle James! How come? Does he kiss better than I do?"

"Don't be disgusting," Heather said quickly, making a face. She turned and stared out of the fogged-up window at her snow-covered front yard. "I was thinking of different ways to kill him."

"Oh. Well. That's healthy," Ben said sarcastically.

He leaned toward her, put his hands gently on the sides of her face, and turned her head back to him. "Kiss me again and maybe you can think up some ways to kill your aunt, too."

Heather reached up and pulled his hands away. They were so warm, and she was so cold. Cold all over.

"Aunt Belle is okay," she said quietly, staring straight ahead at the steamy windshield. "I think she must hate my uncle as much as I do. She's just too afraid of him to admit it."

Ben didn't reply. He took her cold hand between his and squeezed it tenderly, trying to warm it up.

Heather suddenly felt guilty. Why had she let her mind wander to her uncle while she was kissing Ben?

Impulsively, she grabbed the back of his neck and pulled him to her, pressing her lips against his.

Without you, I'd be so lonely, she thought.

Without you, I'd be so sad.

And yet, her mind wandered when she kissed him. Some of the old excitement was gone. Was she growing tired of Ben?

No. It's just my bad mood, she decided.

It's just that I hate Uncle James *so much* it's ruining my feelings for everyone else.

Still holding the back of Ben's neck, she kissed him hungrily.

"Oh!"

The loud noise right by her head startled her. She jumped back in her seat, her heart pounding.

It took her a while to realize what was happening. Someone was standing outside the car, hitting the passenger window.

Uncle James!

Chapter 3

"Uncle James!"

He was tapping hard on the glass with the wooden handle of the snow shovel.

Through the fogged window, Heather could see that his narrow face was bright red with anger, his eyes nearly popping out of his head from behind the thick, metal-rimmed eyeglasses he always wore. His thin lips were pulled back, revealing the yellowed false teeth that made Heather sick every time she saw them.

"Hey — what's his problem?" Ben asked, letting go of Heather and edging back to his side of the car.

"Leave us alone!" Heather started to scream. But before she could get the words out, her uncle pulled open the car door, and she nearly toppled out into the snow.

"Hey — let go!"

Uncle James grabbed the elbow of her jacket and tugged. "I've been calling you for twenty minutes. I *know* you heard me!"

"No, we couldn't — " Ben started.

But Heather knew better than to resist when her uncle was this angry. She allowed him to pull her from the car, then jerked her arm away and stood facing him, determined not to cry or be upset.

"What do you want, Uncle James?" she asked coldly, reaching up to straighten her blonde pony-tail.

"Don't you care what the neighbors think?" he asked, his voice high, excited, his face still red. He had tossed on a bright yellow down ski jacket over the flannel shirt and baggy brown corduroys he always wore.

He's so ridiculous-looking, Heather thought scornfully. In that yellow down parka, he looks like a pencil with a red eraser at the top!

She didn't answer him, just stared at him, aiming all of her hatred toward him, wanting him to wither away and disappear, to melt under the heat of her strong feelings.

"Well, even if *you* don't care what the neighbors think, I do!" he said, angrily tossing the snow shovel halfway across the front yard. "Parked here like a tramp in broad daylight — "

"We weren't doing anything," Heather said.

"Mr. Dickson, I'm really sorry if — " Ben called, leaning across the passenger seat, sticking his head through the open doorway.

"It's time for you to go to work," Uncle James said, ignoring Ben, simply acting as if he were invisible. "If you can tear yourself away from loverboy long enough, maybe you'll get to your job on time for once."

"I'm never late for my job," she muttered.

Her job. Waitress at the Cook's Kitchen Coffee Shop at the mall. It was such a boring, terrible job. And it took up so much of her time and made it so hard for her to keep up with her schoolwork.

And why did she have to have a job? Her parents had left her a ton of money in a trust fund — a trust fund Uncle James wouldn't let her touch.

Uncle James believed in hard work.

He was teaching her to be responsible.

He was teaching her to have self-discipline.

What a joke.

He was deliberately making her life hard and miserable, as he had ever since she was three and her parents had died in that awful car crash, and she had been sent to live with him and Aunt Belle.

Thirteen years ago.

Thirteen years of being taught lessons by Uncle James.

Thirteen years of being embarrassed by him.

Thirteen years of being afraid of him.

Thirteen years of hating him.

"Heather, I'll call you later," Ben said. He had climbed out of the car and was walking around the passenger side to close the door.

"I'll be at the mall till nine," Heather sighed.

Jamming her hands into her jeans pockets, she turned and followed her uncle, who was already crunching over the snow to the house.

I hate you, I hate you, I hate you, she thought.

As if reading her thoughts, he turned suddenly. She saw that he had an odd smile on his face. The lowering afternoon sun reflected off his thick glasses. His face seemed to glow bright yellow.

He's not looking at me. He's looking past me.

He's watching Ben back down the drive, Heather realized. He's smiling because he's celebrating a victory.

He's so happy because he interrupted us. And he totally embarrassed me.

She gripped the pocket lighter in her right pocket and squeezed it hard. The plastic lighter had been her father's. She carried it with her wherever she went.

It wasn't a good luck charm. To Heather's mind, she hadn't had much good luck. But it was somehow comforting to have something that her father had carried and held.

Daddy, if only you knew what Uncle James was really like, you never would have made him my guardian.

"I hate you!"

Uncle James spun around, his features pulled tight in anger.

"Oh." Heather hadn't meant to scream it aloud. It had just slipped out.

"You're a very disturbed young lady," her uncle

said in his scratchy, high-pitched, almost womanly voice. He clenched and unclenched his big, bony hands, staring hard at her. "Very disturbed," he repeated, turning and hurrying to the house. "You need help, young lady. You really do."

Chapter 4

The Cook's Kitchen Coffee Shop was a long, narrow restaurant located between two shoe stores at the Twin Valley Shopping Mall. A long, white Formica counter ran the length of the restaurant with thirty-two red vinyl stools lined up along it.

Heather knew just how many stools there were. She had counted them many times when the restaurant was nearly empty and she was bored.

Eight red vinyl booths with tables, each booth wide enough to seat six people, ran along the wall across from the counter. A girl named Marjorie, who really couldn't chew gum and talk at the same time, was waitress for the counter. The booths were Heather's responsibility.

"Hi, how's it going?" Heather said to Mel Heatter, the cook and manager, as she straightened her black-and-white uniform, tying the white Cook's

Kitchen apron behind her. He looked at his watch in reply.

Okay, okay. I'm ten minutes late. Big deal, Heather thought.

She hated the way Mel looked at his watch every time she arrived. And she hated the stupid uniform. It was so coarse and ugly and made her look and feel forty years old.

"Hi, kid," Marjorie said, nearly choking on her gum.

Heather gave her a little wave. She hated the way Marjorie called her kid.

She hated the smell of grease that she couldn't wash out of her hair. She hated the customers who were always in a hurry, who were always unhappy because their food wasn't good. She hated the greasy quarters they slid under the plates for her, her tips.

Why do they come here if they want good food? Heather wondered.

But mainly she hated the fact that this job took up so much of her time, kept her from studying, from seeing friends, from seeing Ben.

And it was so unnecessary.

A tired-looking couple, dressed in identical gray down jackets, pulling a reluctant little boy with a runny nose, made their way to the back booth. Heather picked up a tray and three glasses, filled them with water, and took them to the table.

The little boy was whining loudly, protesting that he wasn't hungry. The mother and father, still in their coats, had picked up menus and were ignoring his pleas.

"Is the fish fresh here?" the woman asked, staring at the menu.

"We only have fish sticks," Heather told her.

The woman made a face. "Then I guess I'll have a cheeseburger," she said.

"I don't want a cheeseburger," the little boy cried, wiping his runny nose with the back of his hand.

"Use your napkin," the father said, studying the menu.

"I'll come back when you've decided," Heather said, and started back toward the front.

"But I don't *want* anything!" the little boy called after her.

"Hi, Heather."

Heather immediately recognized the hoarse, squeaky voice. She was surprised to see her friend Kim Slater standing at the counter. Kim was short and a little chunky, and the three long, bulky sweaters she had chosen to wear, one on top of the other, made her look nearly round.

"Kim — hi!" Heather cried, happy to see her. She looked behind the counter to the kitchen to see if Mel was watching. He wasn't. He was back by the dishwasher. "How'd you know I was here?"

"I called your house," Kim said, starting to stuff her gloves into a coat pocket and then remembering she wasn't wearing a coat. "Your uncle must've been in a bad mood or something."

"So what else is new?" Heather muttered, adjusting her ponytail. "What did he say to you?"

"He started yelling at me about how I shouldn't call and disturb him when you weren't home. But how am I supposed to know if you're home unless I call?"

"He's angry at me," Heather said, then quickly added, "for a change. He caught Ben and me kissing in the driveway."

"Kissing? He gets angry about *kissing*?" Kim laughed her high squeaky laugh. "What would he do if he caught you *really* making out? Have a heart attack?"

"I wish," Heather said glumly. She looked again to make sure Mel wasn't watching. He didn't like it when his waitresses talked to friends, even if they weren't busy.

"We're ready to order now," the man in the back booth called, loud enough for Mel to poke his head out of the kitchen to see if Heather was being negligent.

"I'll be right back," Heather told Kim. "You want something to eat or anything?"

Kim shook her head. "Not in *this* dive," she said in her hoarse, funny voice.

Heather hurried over and took the family's order. Three cheeseburgers, three french fries, three Cokes. The man acted as if he'd been waiting for hours. "I don't want mine too juicy," he said.

No problem. I'll dry it off for you, Heather thought.

She scribbled the order onto her pad and shoved it onto the kitchen window shelf for Mel. He muttered something unintelligible, and Heather returned to Kim, who was leaning against the counter, watching Marjorie chew gum.

"I wish I could quit this stupid job," Heather sighed.

"Well, why don't you? You don't need the money, do you?" Kim asked.

"No. I don't. I have three thousand dollars in my checking account."

"So quit. Go ahead. Quit right now. Then you can come over to my house."

"I can't," Heather said, straightening the napkins in a metal dispenser. "My stupid uncle won't let me spend that money."

"What do you mean? It's *yours*, isn't it?"

"Uncle James says I have to save it."

"Save it for what?"

"He won't say. Just save it. Oh, I hate him so much!" Heather said, and then lowered her voice because Marjorie was staring at her. "He won't let me spend it on clothes, or lunches, or school expenses — or anything. So I have to work."

"You told me you have a trust fund, right?" Kim was struggling to understand Uncle James's reasoning. "With enough money to pay for college?"

"More than enough. I'm loaded," Heather said. "But I can't touch any of my money. Uncle James is in charge of it until I'm eighteen. And he wants me to work to build my character."

"What a creep," Kim said, shaking her brown curls.

"He's worse than a creep," Heather confided. "I think he's spending some of my money. He bought a new computer last week for his study. I saw the receipt. He paid cash for it. He doesn't have that kind of money."

"Can you prove he's taking your money?" Kim asked in a loud whisper. "If you can — "

"I can't," Heather said. "I don't even know where he keeps the bank records. There's no way I can prove anything. I just have a hunch."

"Well, you should — " Kim started.

"Hey — you've got customers!" Mel barked angrily.

Heather turned to the booths. Two elderly women were easing themselves into a booth. One of them was struggling to prop her cane against the back of the booth.

"Later," Kim said, heading toward the door. "Call me, okay?"

"Yeah. Okay," Heather called back to her, hurrying over to help the two women.

She was nearly to their booth when a hand reached out and grabbed her arm.

Chapter 5

"Oh. Sorry. I didn't mean to scare you."

Heather stared at the boy, waiting for her heart to stop pounding. He had the most amazing hair. It was pure white. Not blond. Not silver. Pure white. It was parted in the middle and fell in waves down to his collar.

It was even more startling because the boy's features were dark. His skin was ruddy, almost tanned. His eyes were dark brown. He had the most adorable cleft in his chin.

Heather just stared at him. He may have been the most handsome boy she had ever seen. He looked like he could be in the movies or on TV.

"I was just trying to get your attention," he said, embarrassed. "I didn't mean to scare you. Really. Are you okay?"

Heather realized she was staring at him with

her mouth wide open. "Sorry. I didn't see you. I mean — "

"Could we have a check, please?" the man in the back booth called impatiently.

"Check please," his little boy repeated.

"Excuse me," Heather told the white-haired boy, and hurried to the back booth, grateful for the interruption.

Get yourself together, she told herself. You've seen good-looking guys before. What's the big deal?

Such amazing hair.

White as snow.

She totaled the check for the family. The little boy had been true to his word. He hadn't tasted the cheeseburger. Then she took the order from the two elderly ladies — two chocolate ice-cream sodas — and handed it in to Mel.

Business was picking up. Several of the counter seats were now filled, and Heather could see that Marjorie was in her usual state of confusion, trying to remember who had ordered what.

"I haven't forgotten you," she said to the boy with the white hair. "Are you ready to order?"

"Yeah, I guess," he said, his large brown eyes peering up at her.

Coffee, tea, or me? she thought.

Now where did *that* come from?!

"I just want a burger and fries," he said. "And a Coke."

"I haven't seen you here before," Heather said, scribbling down the order.

"I just moved to Twin Valley a couple of weeks ago," he said, unbuttoning his denim jacket. He wore a navy blue sweatshirt underneath. "You go to Twin Valley High?"

"Yeah," Heather said, looking back to see if the ice-cream sodas were ready. "You, too?" He nodded. "What homeroom are you in?"

He thought about it and laughed. His eyes crinkled when he laughed. Heather was a real sucker for crinkly eyes. "I can't remember his name. You know — the tall teacher."

"Mr. Louper?"

"Yeah. Louper," he said, spinning the salt shaker between his hands.

"Isn't that a sophomore homeroom?" Heather asked, checking to make sure Mel wasn't watching. She wasn't allowed to chat this long with the customers.

"I *thought* everyone looked really young!" he exclaimed.

They both laughed.

"What's your name?" he asked.

"Heather. Heather Dickson."

"You look like a Heather," he said, his face expressionless.

"What do you mean?"

"You know. All blonde and pretty. Heathery." He smiled.

"Thanks. I guess. What's your name?" She looked down the row to see three teenage boys climb into the front booth. One of them kept punching his friend playfully on the shoulder.

"Snowman," he said.

"That's your name?"

"Well, it's what people call me."

"Why?" Heather asked. "Because of your hair?"

"No." He flashed her another smile. "Because I'm *cold as ice*." He raised his hand for her to slap him five.

She ignored it and took a step back. "Snowman?"

He shrugged. "It's just a dumb nickname." He made a funny face, then stared into her eyes. His eyes seemed to glow like dark coals beneath the white hair.

He wasn't just looking at her, checking her out, Heather felt. She thought she could read a plea in his eyes. He seemed to be asking her for something.

Now, don't get carried away, she scolded herself.

"I think of snowmen as being very round and very soft," she said.

"That's me," he said.

He's so good-looking, Heather thought. I wonder if he realizes how incredibly handsome he is.

She turned away to stop herself from staring at him. "I'll put your order in," she said, and headed toward the kitchen.

It was very busy for a Thursday night. All of

the booths were filled, which meant that Heather had to run in six directions at once. It also meant that she couldn't stop to chat any further with Snowman.

As she worked, she kept looking over to his booth where he was hungrily devouring his food. She realized she felt drawn to him. It wasn't just that he was so unusual-looking with that white hair. He also seemed like a really nice guy.

He had looked disappointed when she had dropped his food on the table and hurried on to the next booth. She could tell he wanted to talk some more.

She could tell he was attracted to her, too.

"You look like a Heather," he had said.

Funny thing to say. But she knew she was pretty, with her golden hair, which she usually swept straight back into an off-centered ponytail, her creamy, pale skin and high cheekbones, and her dark blue, almost-violet eyes.

She could be really popular, she knew. If she weren't so shy. If she didn't have to spend so much time working in this awful restaurant.

If Uncle James didn't restrict her from doing anything that was fun.

When she dropped a tray of water glasses and the glass shattered about her feet, she looked over at him. He gave her a sympathetic look, then returned to his food.

Mel yelled something from the kitchen. Marjorie

offered to help clean up the glass. Customers called from three different booths at once.

She couldn't stop thinking about Snowman.

He must be pretty lonely, she figured, having just moved to Twin Valley.

I'll have to look for him in school, she thought.

She walked over to his booth, pad in hand. She wanted to say something to him. But her mind was suddenly a blank. She couldn't think of a thing.

He looked at her again with those searching, dark eyes.

"Ready for the check?" That was the only thing she could think of to say.

Why did this always happen to her when she became nervous? Why did she always get so tongue-tied?

He took the check from her and reached into his back pocket for his wallet. "Whose homeroom are you in?" he asked.

"Oh. Uh . . ." She was so startled by the question, she couldn't think of it. "Reedy. Mr. Reedy. 304."

"Yeah? I'll look for you," he said, smiling up at her. "I don't know too many kids."

His smile faded abruptly.

He pulled himself up in the booth and reached into his other jeans pockets. He suddenly looked upset. He reached quickly into his jacket pockets.

"Oh, no," he said, blushing.

That's really cute, Heather thought. He looks just like a ten-year-old when he blushes like that.

"My wallet," he said. "I must've left it at home." He searched through all of his pockets again, then looked to see if it had fallen on the floor.

"Can't find it?" she asked. What a stupid question. Of *course* he couldn't find it. Why else would he continue searching like that?

"I — I don't have any money," he said, dropping back down onto the vinyl seat. "Does this mean you have to arrest me?"

He looked so worried, Heather couldn't help but laugh.

"I could wash dishes, I guess," he said. He looked so serious, Heather couldn't tell if he was kidding or not.

"Why don't I pay for your food?" Heather told him, checking to see where Mel was. "And you can pay me back tomorrow morning in school."

"Oh, wow. That's really nice of you," he said, relaxing a bit. "I could drive home and get my wallet, and come back."

Heather glanced up at the clock. "No. It's almost closing time. Just pay me back tomorrow morning, Snowman."

"That's really great of you," he said, climbing quickly out of the booth. She was surprised to see that he was nearly a foot taller than she. "I've got another idea," he said, buttoning his faded denim jacket. "Why don't I pay you back Saturday night? We can go dancing or something."

Yes! Heather thought.

But she forced herself to be cautious. "Well . . . I usually don't go out with customers," she said, hating the way the words sounded.

"But I'm *not* a customer," he insisted. "At least I'm not a *paying* customer!"

They both laughed.

He's really sweet, she thought.

"I'll bet you get hit on a lot," he said.

"Yeah. Sometimes. You should *see* the kind of guys I attract!"

"Well . . . okay. I'll pay you back in school tomorrow," he said, looking away.

"No! I mean — I'll go out with you. Saturday night is fine."

Now I sound too eager, she thought.

But what difference did it make? She wanted to go out with him. He seemed like someone really special.

"Hey, Heather — you on vacation?" Mel called, sticking his sweaty bald head out through the kitchen door.

Heather scribbled her address on her pad, tore off the sheet, and handed it to Snowman.

"Thanks again," he said, and headed to the door, taking long strides, his hair glowing under the bright overhead lights.

Heather had trouble concentrating on anything for the rest of her shift. Luckily there was only about twenty minutes to go.

"What a night!" Marjorie exclaimed as Heather

pulled on her jacket and punched the time clock. "My head is still spinning!"

"See you tomorrow," Heather said and stepped out into the cold, thinking about Snowman.

"Now, where did I park the car?" she asked herself, surveying the endless parking lot. It had snowed while she had been working. Another inch added to the six inches already on the ground. Most of the cars were blanketed with a thin layer of white.

It looks pretty, she thought.

Everything looks pretty tonight. Even this parking lot.

She remembered that she had parked down by the movie theater. Pulling up the collar of her down jacket, she lowered her head against the onrushing wind and began walking.

One by one, the store lights went out. Each store seemed to darken as she passed. She had the eerie feeling that she was causing them to go out.

The parking lot seemed to grow darker. She turned a corner and picked up her pace. Her breath floated up in gray clouds against the black, moonless sky.

Her sneakers slid on the slushy snow. She tried to remember why she had parked so far from the restaurant.

This area of the parking lot was nearly deserted. The last show at the movie theater had started. There were only a few cars parked by the entrance.

It was eerily quiet. She never liked the parking

lot after the mall had closed. It was too large, too dark, too empty. It made her feel so vulnerable.

She stopped when she heard footsteps behind her. Soft footsteps in the fresh, wet snow.

Fast.

Faster.

Coming toward her.

"Oh." She uttered a low cry and started to run.

Someone was following her.

Chapter 6

Heather took a deep breath and spun around.

"Ben!"

"Hi, Heather." He came jogging up to her, his work boots squishing in the wet snow.

"You scared me." Her heart was refusing to slow back down to its normal rhythm.

"Sorry. I thought you heard me calling to you." He smiled at her and put his arm around her shoulder. He was wearing his blue down jacket and had a blue wool ski cap pulled down over his ears. "Hey — you're shaking."

"You — you really frightened me," Heather stammered. "The parking lot is so dark here, and when I heard the footsteps behind me — "

"You have too much imagination," Ben said.

"Now you sound like my uncle." She said it with more anger than she had intended. "He's always putting me down for having an imagination. As if that's the worst thing in the world a person could have. I think he does it because he doesn't have any imagination at all."

"Sure he does," Ben said playfully. "He has a dirty mind, doesn't he?"

Heather frowned and gave Ben a shove. "That's not imagination. Don't be such a creep." Her car was a few yards ahead of them. "What are you doing here, anyway? How did you get here?"

"Walked."

"You walked in the cold? All the way to the mall? That's not like you."

"Hey, I just wanted to see you — okay? Why are you giving me a hard time?"

Heather knew why she was giving Ben a hard time. Snowman. She felt guilty about making the date with Snowman.

She also wanted some time to think about Snowman. She didn't want to have to talk to Ben now.

"Sorry," she said softly, pulling open the car door. "Come on. Get in. I'll drive you home."

He climbed into the passenger seat and struggled to get the seat belt to click in.

"You don't have to make such a fuss with the seat belt. I'm not *that* bad of a driver," Heather said irritably.

"Yes, you are," he said, laughing. He finally managed to get it to click.

"So why are you here?" she asked, searching her jacket pocket for the key.

"Stop being so friendly," he said sarcastically.

He slid down in the seat and put his knee up on the dashboard in front of him. "I felt bad about this afternoon. You know. About your uncle and everything. So I came to see how you were doing."

Why is he being so sweet? Heather thought. It's almost as if he knows about Snowman, and he's come to make me feel bad.

"I'm okay," she said, turning the key, pumping the gas pedal. The car started right up. She turned on the windshield wipers. They scraped across the glass, pushing away the wet covering of snow.

"It was pretty embarrassing," Ben said, staring straight ahead at the scraping wipers. "I mean, the way he dragged you out of the car. It was like some bad TV show or something."

"I just want to murder him when he does things like that," Heather said, backing out of the parking spot. "I try to be cool about it. I mean, I should be used to it by now, right? But I can't help myself. I just lose it."

"I thought you were pretty cool," he said, turning to her, reaching out, and giving her ponytail a gentle, affectionate tug.

"He just thinks I'm an object, a belonging of his," Heather said heatedly. "He thinks he can do anything he wants, say anything he wants. In front of anybody. He doesn't care about me at all. Or my feelings. He doesn't care if he embarrasses me in front of my friends. That was so humiliating what he did this afternoon!"

"Maybe we'll laugh about it some day," Ben said.

"You know. Like in a hundred years or so."

She laughed. Ben could always make her laugh.

So why was she going out with a stranger on Saturday night?

Just because he was a stranger? Just because he wasn't Ben?

Am I really that tired of Ben? she asked herself.

No. Not really. . . .

"What are you thinking about?" Ben asked, holding onto the door handle as she slid around a corner.

The car bumped hard against the high curb. The bump seemed to shake all thoughts from her head. "Uh . . . nothing," she said. "Just driving."

"Well, what do you want to do Saturday night?" he asked. "Jerry's parents are going to be away, so he's having a party. A real blowout, he says. You know Jerry. That probably means he'll have a can of beer for everyone to pass around and take a sip!"

He laughed, expecting her to join in. But she didn't.

She was concentrating on coming up with an excuse for Saturday night.

"Uh . . . why don't you go to Jerry's party?"

He looked confused. "Without you?"

"Yeah. I . . . uh . . . can't go out Saturday night." She turned another corner, carefully this time, onto Hedgerow Drive, Ben's street.

"Because of your uncle? Did he ground you because of this afternoon?"

"No. We . . . uh . . . have to go visit these people.

Cousins. My aunt's cousins. They insisted I come along."

Wow, am I a bad liar! Heather thought. I can't even make it sound *halfway* believable.

"Oh, I see."

Ben wasn't buying it. That was pretty obvious. She had to make him believe it, she decided. Why make him feel bad? Why make him suspicious?

"Would you like to come visit the cousins with me?" she asked. A sudden inspiration. "It wouldn't be any fun, but at least we'd be together."

"How would your uncle feel about that?" Ben asked unhappily.

"Yeah. I guess you're right," Heather said, pulling into his drive, the tires skidding up the low slope. "But it might be fun to bring you along just to make him angry."

"No, it wouldn't," Ben said quietly. "He'd probably throw me out of the car while it was moving or something. Your uncle isn't too subtle."

"Tell me about it," Heather said bitterly. She yawned. "Get out, okay? I'm tired, I can't see straight. This stupid job — "

"Okay, okay. I can take a hint," Ben said, struggling to unclick the seat belt.

Heather felt bad. She didn't like hurting him. She didn't like disappointing him.

She had so few friends, she didn't like disappointing any of them.

"Hey," she said, smiling playfully. She leaned

over, covered his hands with hers, and kissed him.

He returned the kiss. Hard, then harder.

His kiss seemed different to her. Needier somehow.

Almost desperate.

Can he read my mind? she wondered, putting her arms around him.

It was a long, passionate kiss.

She couldn't help it.

She couldn't control it.

All the while she was thinking about Snowman.

Chapter 7

Everything glowed silver-white. Then a tall pine tree, its branches dark shadows beneath a covering of snow, came into focus.

The snow-covered hill sloped steeply at her feet. Heather raised a mittened hand to her forehead to shield her eyes. Her breath came out in little puffs of white against the aqua sky. Her bright red boots crunched noisily over the deep snow.

Despite the snow, the air was warm. She was wearing her down jacket unzipped. A long red wool scarf was wrapped several times around her neck.

She stepped up to the sled. It was an old-fashioned wooden sled with red metal runners and the words *American Flyer* stenciled in red on the wood.

Such a beautiful day for sledding, she thought. A perfect day. Why am I the only one on the hill?

A blue shadow moved in front of her path on the

snow. She felt a sudden chill in the air. The shadow was long and lean, a dark blot on the pure, sparkling snow.

Heather turned around to see who was making the shadow.

"Uncle James!"

He stared at her, then down at the sled.

He was wearing the yellow ski jacket and the same baggy brown corduroys, one trouser leg over his boot, one leg under. The sun filled his thick eyeglasses with bright golden light. She couldn't see his eyes.

"Uncle James — what are you doing up here?"

"Do you know how to sled?" he asked.

"Yeah. Sure," she said. Then she added to herself, No thanks to you.

He had never taken her sledding. Not once.

He had never taken her anywhere, had never played with her, or taken her to the movies, or done any of the normal things fathers did with daughters.

He had no interest in entertaining her.

He kicked at the back of the sled with his black rubber boot. It slid forward a few inches.

"Let me see you sled," he said.

"What?"

"It's a perfect day, Heather. A perfect day for sledding."

She stared at him, surprised by the request. She still couldn't see his eyes. The sun reflected in the glass lenses acted as a shield.

"Okay," she said. She loved sledding. She loved

the ease of it, the feel of gliding so softly, so gracefully.

It was so easy, it wasn't like real life at all.

It was always like sliding through a soft, white dream.

She bent down and grabbed the wooden sled rudder. Then she dropped easily onto her stomach on the sled. "Give me a push?" she asked, turning her head back to see her uncle.

"No," he said.

"What?"

"No. Don't lie down. Sit up. I want to ride, too."

"You want to sled with me?"

He nodded his narrow head. He looks like a toothpick.

Is he as brittle as a toothpick? As fragile?

She pulled herself up, slid around. Now she was sitting in the front. "Climb on, Uncle James," she said. "Plenty of room."

It took him forever to lower himself onto the sled and arrange his long legs behind her. "Hold onto my waist," she said.

His grip was hesitant, light. It felt strange to have him holding onto her like that. In all the time she had spent growing up in his house, he'd never touched her, except by accident.

Except for the times he had slapped her face in anger.

She gripped the sides of the sled. The snow sparkled as if millions of tiny diamonds were embedded in it. It became so bright, she closed her eyes.

"Ready?" she called back to him.

"Ready," he replied, tightening his grip on her waist.

She leaned forward, moving her weight toward the front of the sled. They began to slide, slowly at first, then picking up speed.

Looking down, the slope of the hill seemed steeper than she remembered. Much steeper.

Perfect, she thought. A perfect day for sledding.

The top of the snow is wet and ice-hard.

So fast. We'll go down so fast.

Like a roller coaster that only goes down, down, down.

So perfect.

"Here we go!" she cried happily.

They were sliding down now, faster, faster, gliding so easily. Heather felt the wind against her face, listened to the quiet whisper of the runners against the snow.

The hill seemed endless.

She couldn't see the bottom. She could only see the onrushing white snow.

But there had to be a bottom, right?

There had to be an end.

They were really speeding now, down, down, plummeting down.

She aimed the sled at the tall pine tree, aimed it dead center at the wide, dark trunk.

They were going so fast, like a speeding train.

A few feet from the tree, Heather leaned to the

right — and jumped off. She rolled onto the snow and kept rolling. So cold. So wet.

So easy.

The loud crack she heard was the sound of her uncle's head hitting the tree trunk.

The impact split his head in two, and his body went flying backward, up high in the air.

Awakening from her dream, Heather sat up in bed and stretched.

Such a vivid dream. She could remember every detail.

She dressed quickly for school and went down to breakfast with a smile on her face.

Chapter 8

"I'm so nervous. I can't decide what to wear," Heather said, wrapping the phone cord around her wrist.

"Well, okay. *I'll* go out with him, then," Kim said on the other end. She giggled her hoarse giggle. "Where are you going?"

"To The Woods."

Across the room, Heather's uncle put down his newspaper and gave her a suspicious look.

"You know. The dance club," Heather added quickly. Her uncle made a sour face and resumed reading his paper.

Heather turned her face to the living room wall and lowered her voice as she talked to Kim. "Uncle James is listening to every word I say," she whispered. "It makes me so mad. He's sitting there pretending to read his newspaper."

"Why don't you get your own phone?" Kim asked.

"He won't let me. He says one phone is enough for a house. Can you imagine? One phone in the living room. I have no privacy, Kim. None at all!"

She hadn't realized she had raised her voice. Her uncle shot her another dirty look. "Could you get off the phone? I can't hear myself think," he called loudly, loudly enough for Kim to hear.

"I just got on," Heather said through gritted teeth, trying to control her temper.

"None of your back talk," he said, pretending to read the paper.

"I've got to go, Kim," Heather said angrily.

"Wear the red top," Kim said. "You know, the silky one. You look great in that one."

"Thanks. 'Bye. I'll call you tomorrow." She replaced the receiver and started up to her room.

"About time you started chipping in on the phone bill," Uncle James said. "You make most of the calls, you know."

"I'll be glad to pay for my own phone," Heather said, stopping at the bottom of the stairs.

He pretended he hadn't heard her.

"Going out again, huh?" he said.

"It *is* Saturday night," Heather said brusquely.

"What about your schoolwork? I don't suppose you've given that any thought?"

Luckily Aunt Belle came in from the kitchen to ask Uncle James a question, giving Heather a chance to escape up the stairs. Thank you, Aunt Belle, she thought, hurrying into her room. One more second of that conversation, and I don't know *what* I would have said!

Saturday nights were always so tense. Uncle James carried on every Saturday before she went out, just trying to get her upset and nervous before her date. And usually succeeding.

"And I do hope this new boyfriend of yours is picking you up at the house," he shouted up the stairs.

"James, let her get dressed," she heard Aunt Belle plead.

But he never listened to her, either. He was even more of a bully to Heather's poor, frail aunt. Always bossing her around, telling her what to do and how to do it, what to wear, treating her like she was his personal slave.

Why does she put up with it? Heather wondered. Because she's so frail, so weak? Sometimes Heather looked through their old photo album at the photos of her aunt and uncle when they were young. Her aunt seemed so much stronger in those photos, so lively and full of spirit.

He's destroyed her, Heather decided. He's just bullied her and bossed her till she has no spirit left at all.

"Well?" he called up the stairs, as she pulled on the silky red top.

"Yes, he's picking me up here," Heather called

down. "You can check him out and make him feel as uncomfortable as everyone else I bring here!"

She had gone too far, and she knew it. It's just that I'm nervous, and he won't leave me alone, she thought.

He muttered something, a string of curses most likely, then shouted, "I'm sick of your smart mouth! I'm not going to take it much longer!"

She forced herself not to reply. She froze, listening to whether he was coming up the stairs to confront her. He loved to draw out arguments, to keep badgering her in his reedy voice. He loved to see her get more and more upset. He never let anything drop.

Heather glanced at the clock on the wall above her desk. It was a little after eight o'clock. Snowman would be there any minute.

Maybe, just maybe she could introduce him to her aunt and uncle and then hurry him out of the house before Uncle James had the time to start an argument with him.

Snowman seemed like such an understanding guy. He had dropped by the restaurant the night before, just before closing. Mel was out back, so Heather slipped Snowman a free plate of french fries and a Coke.

When she told him it was a rule of her uncle's that he had to meet every boy Heather went out with, Snowman told her not to look so worried. He had no problem with coming to her house. "I know how to handle adults," he had said, his dark eyes staring confidently into hers.

"My uncle is real difficult," she had said.

"No problem," Snowman repeated, gobbling the french fries hungrily one after the other. "I'll have him eating right here," he said, holding up the palm of his right hand.

Heather laughed bitterly. "You don't know my uncle." Then she turned and saw Mel glaring at her from the window to the kitchen, so she hurried to clear away some booths.

When she looked back, Snowman was gone. In place of a tip, he had left a folded-up piece of paper beside the plate. Heather put down the stack of dirty dishes she was carrying, picked up the paper, and unfolded it.

Drawn in pencil was a snowman, just two circles, with a top hat and a smiling face. And beside the snowman was a little heart.

How sweet, Heather thought, folding up the piece of paper and tucking it into the pocket of her skirt. What a nice tip.

Thinking about it now brought a smile to her face. She finished brushing her hair and glanced at the clock for the nine-thousandth time. It was ten after eight.

She nervously squeezed the plastic butane lighter in her hand, twirling it in her fingers, waiting for the doorbell to ring.

And there it was.

Even though she was waiting for it, the doorbell's loud ring made her jump.

She tossed the lighter into her bag, then hurried down the stairs, hoping to get to the front door before her uncle.

But she wasn't fast enough.

Uncle James was already opening the door.

Chapter 9

Heather stopped two thirds of the way down the stairs, her heart pounding. Uncle James had pulled open the front door and was staring through the storm door at Snowman, a look of undisguised displeasure on his face.

"Are *you* Heather's date?" he asked, as if he couldn't believe what he was seeing. He still hadn't opened the storm door. Poor Snowman was standing out in the cold.

"For goodness' sake, let him in!" Heather cried, hurrying down the last few stairs and pushing past her uncle to open the storm door.

A blast of cold air accompanied Snowman into the room. "Hi," he said, smiling at her. He was wearing a fifties-style oversized gray wool overcoat. He stamped the snow off his boots.

"Close the door. You're letting out all the heat," her uncle complained, looking Snowman up and down.

"This is my uncle James," Heather said, pushing the front door closed. As if you haven't guessed, she thought. "I — I'll get my coat." And maybe we can get out of here fast before Uncle James starts anything.

"I didn't catch *your* name," her uncle said to Snowman, suspicion in his voice.

Heather realized she didn't know his real name. She only knew him as Snowman.

She started to say something, but Snowman spoke up first. "It's Bill," he said, looking at Heather. "Bill Jeffers."

"Jeffers? What kind of a name is that?" Uncle James asked loudly. "You Hungarian?"

"No." Snowman gave him a pleasant smile. "There's a little bit of everything in my family, I guess. I don't really know where we're from."

"Just a mutt," Uncle James said under his breath.

Heather pulled on her coat. She started to tug Snowman toward the door, but Aunt Belle came into the room.

She looks so tired, Heather thought. She's only forty-five, but she looks much older. Her once-bright copper hair was now mostly gray. "This is my aunt Belle," Heather said quickly.

"It's nice to meet you." Her aunt extended her tiny hand and Snowman shook it.

"Look at his hair," Uncle James said to Aunt Belle, snickering. "Ever see a young guy with white hair like that?" He turned back to Snowman. "Guess you've got a lot of worries, huh?"

"Stop it, James," scolded Heather's aunt. "You're embarrassing him."

"That's okay," Snowman said, giving her a warm smile. "I'm used to a lot of kidding. I've had this white hair my whole life."

"Some kind of albino," Uncle James muttered.

"Hush up," Aunt Belle told him. Strong words for her. Heather could tell that she liked Snowman.

"I really like your house," Snowman said, looking around the living room. "It looks so comfortable, like a real family lives here."

Aunt Belle beamed. "Well, I try to make it a real home for all of us."

"Is that your car?" Uncle James asked, staring out the living room window to the driveway where a black Toyota Celica was parked.

"No. Actually, I borrowed it from a friend."

"Don't have your own, huh?" Uncle James asked. He made the question sound like an accusation.

"My family just moved here a short while ago," Snowman said. "We haven't had time to buy a new car."

"What does your father do?" Uncle James demanded.

"Uncle James — please!" Heather cried angrily. Then she softened it by saying, "Bill and I are going to be late."

"My father isn't alive," Snowman said, pushing back his thick, white hair with one hand, his face becoming an expressionless blank.

Uncle James just stared at him in silence, his eyes cold, unfeeling.

"That's too bad," Aunt Belle said uncomfortably. She fussed with the collar of her housedress.

"Come on, Bill. Let's go." Heather tugged open the front door.

"It was very nice meeting you both," Snowman said. "I'll get Heather back nice and early. Hope to see you again."

He *really* does know how to talk to adults, Heather thought admiringly. Maybe Uncle James has met his match here. Maybe Snowman can manage to outcharm him!

"What should I say if Ben calls?" Uncle James asked, a thin-lipped smile on his face.

"What?" His question startled her. It was so unexpected.

"What should I say if your boyfriend calls?" Uncle James said. "You remember Ben, don't you?"

Heather could feel her face turning bright red.

Uncle James knew just how to embarrass her.

Why was he doing this? Why did he want to upset her, make her feel bad?

Why did he hate her so much?

"James, I really don't think — " Aunt Belle started.

"Shut up!" Uncle James snapped, turning an angry glance on his wife.

"Good night," Heather said disgustedly, and pulled Snowman out the door.

The cold night air felt good on her face. She took his arm as they headed down the drive to the car. "Wow," she said softly, shaking her head, still agitated over her uncle's deliberate thoughtlessness. "Wow."

"He's a lot of laughs," Snowman said sarcastically.

"I warned you about him," Heather said. And then she quickly added, "You're not upset or anything? I mean, about him."

She pulled open the passenger door and climbed in. It was colder inside the car. The seats were ice-cold. The car smelled of oranges.

Snowman slid behind the wheel and slammed the door. "He's no problem," he said, reaching into the overcoat pocket for the ignition key. "Really. My dad was a lot like that. Only worse."

"Really?" Heather shifted in the seat, shivering. "Worse than Uncle James?"

"Yeah," Snowman said, starting up the car. "But I handled him." He winked at her. "I guess I can handle your uncle."

"Well, you were very good in there," Heather said. "Uncle James tried to insult you. But you just wouldn't let him get under your skin."

"I told you, Heather. Adults are no problem for me. I really can handle them."

"Well, I think my aunt is in love with you already.

What you said about the house must have made her day. She works so hard to keep the house really nice, and it isn't easy because Uncle James won't let her spend a nickel."

"Let's not talk about them tonight," Snowman said, backing down the drive. "Let's just party, okay?"

"Sounds good," Heather said, settling back in the low seat. "Could we have some heat?"

"Yeah. Sure." As he drove down the street, he fumbled with the dashboard controls. "I just have to find it."

"You don't know where the heat control is?" She leaned forward to help him. Her hand landed on his. She left it there for a few moments. His hand was very warm.

"I told you. I borrowed the car. From a friend. Hey — here it is." He slid a dial to the right. "The heat should come up soon."

A few seconds later, the air from the heater started to warm up. He turned onto Park Drive, the car moving silently past snowy yards, the headlights bright white against the night sky.

"Still want to go to The Woods?" he asked.

"Yeah, sure. If you want to. Are you a good dancer?"

"The best," he said, grinning at her.

"Well, at least you're modest."

"Actually, I was lying. I dance like a water buffalo on roller skates."

"I've never seen a water buffalo on roller skates," Heather said.

"Well, you will tonight." He pressed down on the gas pedal and the car spurted forward, its tires protesting at first, sliding on a patch of icy road.

They talked easily, aimlessly for a while, about the town, about school. Heather found herself doing most of the talking.

I feel so comfortable with him, she thought. I can't believe I was so nervous before he arrived.

She turned, leaning against the door, and took a long look at him. Passing streetlights made his hair seem to blink on and off, white then black, white then black. The changing light made his brown eyes seem to flicker with his hair. They looked dark and intense staring straight ahead as they followed the twin headlight beams.

He's really great-looking, Heather thought. I even like the cleft in his chin. She wondered what it would be like to kiss him, to wrap her hands in his thick, white hair. The blowing heat made her feel warm and dreamy. It was so cozy in the car now, so cozy sitting beside Snowman, watching the dark houses roll past.

Suddenly Snowman's expression changed. He looked in the rearview mirror. It filled with light. He looked away, then looked again.

"Whoa," he said quietly, his eyes narrowing as he stared into the mirror. He pushed down hard on the gas. The car uttered a loud roar and sped forward.

Heather sank back into the seat. "Snowman — what's wrong?"

He checked the mirror again, his face not revealing any emotion at all. "I think we're being followed."

Chapter 10

The light in the rearview mirror seemed to get brighter.

Light filled the car, as if someone had thrown a spotlight onto it.

Snowman made a sharp right, the tires squealing. His eyes kept darting from the windshield to the mirror. His face still revealed no emotion, no tension.

Heather's first thought was that it was Ben. Ben had been terribly upset that Heather wasn't going out with him tonight, she remembered. And her excuse had been pretty lame.

Maybe Ben suspected that she was going out with someone else. But did that mean he would spy on her? Follow her and her date?

That didn't sound like Ben. He wasn't the most secure guy in the world. But he wasn't *crazy*.

"Who is it?" she asked, gripping the door handle with one hand and the bottom of the seat with her other. "Are you *sure* they're following us?"

Snowman, his eyes intent on the road, didn't answer. The street was icy and slick. The car slid. Snowman turned the wheel in the direction of the slide, pulling them out of it just before they slammed into the side of a station wagon parked at the curb.

Heather closed her eyes. She realized she'd been holding her breath. She opened her eyes, surprised to see Snowman still calm, still "cold as ice."

The light from the headlights behind them still filled the car, making Snowman's white hair seem to glow. He roared through a stop sign and made the next left, the car squealing into the narrow street lined with low, dark houses.

It took Heather a little while to realize that the headlights were gone. Snowman had slowed down. He glanced at her and shrugged.

"What happened?" she asked, reluctantly releasing her grip on the door handle.

"Sorry," he said quietly.

"Huh? What do you mean?"

"Guess I've been watching too many bad TV shows."

"You mean — "

He had a very sheepish look on his face. "I mean I don't think we were being followed."

Heather slumped back in the seat, her heart still pounding. She couldn't decide whether to laugh or be furious. "Do you always think people are after you?" she asked.

He shook his head. He turned left again and headed to River Road, where The Woods was located just out of town.

"What made you think we were being followed?" Heather asked. "Is someone following you for some reason? Have you been followed before?"

He laughed. "Maybe it was a friend of *yours*, Heather. There's no one after me. Maybe it was an angry customer from your restaurant, someone you spilled soup on."

"I haven't spilled soup on anyone in weeks," Heather said, pretending to be offended by the idea.

"Well, maybe it was your uncle James, checking up on my driving skills."

Heather made a face and shoved his shoulder playfully.

"Hey — I'm trying to drive!" he protested. "Give me a break!"

"You give *me* a break," Heather said. "You scared me to death — for no reason."

He grinned. His dark eyes seemed to grin, too. "I just don't want you to think I'm boring."

"Come on," Heather demanded. "Did you really think we were being followed or not?"

He slowed down for a traffic light. "Whoever it was was right on my tail," he said, getting serious. "And the headlights were so bright. I guess he had his brights on. He was keeping so close to us, I guess I — I guess I just lost it for a moment."

He looked really embarrassed now. Heather decided she'd better stop questioning him.

She turned and looked out the window. The houses had given way to wide, empty fields. They were nearly out of town.

"What's that in your hand?" he asked.

Heather looked down, surprised. She hadn't even realized she was holding her father's lighter. She held it up. "Just a lighter. It belonged to my father. I keep it as a good luck charm."

"You don't smoke — do you?"

"No. I don't even think it works. It's just . . . well . . . he didn't leave me much. My parents were killed when I was three. I don't really remember them."

Snowman didn't reply. They drove on in silence.

Well, Heather, you certainly know how to end a conversation! she thought, scolding herself for being so grim. "Your dad is dead, too?" she blurted out, remembering his conversation with her uncle.

"Yeah. He didn't even leave me a lighter." His words were bitter, but his face didn't reveal any hard feelings. "Which brings up a difficult subject."

"What's that?" Heather asked.

"Well . . . uh . . . are you sure you want to go dancing? Maybe we could just hang out somewhere and talk or something."

"I've got plenty of money," Heather said quickly, realizing at once what his problem was. "I just got paid yesterday."

"Well, how about if we go half and half?" he asked, looking uncomfortable. "I'm really sorry. I just don't — "

"No problem," she interrupted, touching his hand. "I don't mind at all. Really."

"My mom and my brother and I — well, we're on a pretty tight budget. You know, since we moved and everything. I'm going to get an after-school job. I just haven't had time yet. But when I do, I'll make it up to you, Heather. Really."

"No problem," Heather repeated. "I don't mind paying my share. It's only fair."

"You've been terrific to me," he said. "Giving me free food and everything. I'll pay you back. Really I will."

"Stop," she said. "Don't say another word about it Let's just have a good time. It doesn't matter to me who pays."

He turned onto the gravel parking lot outside The Woods. The lot was nearly filled with cars. Even through the closed car windows Heather could hear the booming rhythm of the music from inside the small dance club.

Snowman parked near the end of the lot, and they stepped out into the cold, crisp night. Heather took a deep breath. "The air smells so fresh," she said, her shoes crunching on the snow-covered gravel. "I love winter. Don't you?"

"Hey, my name is Snowman, right? I've *got* to love winter!"

He took her hand and led her into the throbbing dance club.

Chapter 11

Heather looked for Snowman before homeroom Monday morning, but he didn't seem to be there.

"Have you seen Snowman?" she asked Liza Holloway, a girl she recognized from chorus.

"Who?"

"Uh . . . Bill. Bill Jeffers. He's a new guy."

Liza shook her head. "No new guys in *this* homeroom."

"He's pretty tall and he has white hair," Heather persisted.

Liza shook her head. "You sure he's supposed to be in here?"

"Well, he said this was his homeroom. But he was probably confused," Heather said.

"Who isn't?"

Heather stepped back out into the crowded, noisy hallway and nearly collided with Ben.

"Fancy meeting you here," he said coldly. He

was wearing black, straight-legged jeans and an oversized maroon sweater. He had his green book bag slung over his shoulder.

"Ben. Hi!"

"Hey, you remember my name. Ten points for you, Heather. Like to try for twenty?"

"Give me a break, Ben. What's your problem? Your mother give you raw meat for breakfast again?"

He didn't laugh. He usually liked it when she cracked a joke like that. He considered it his effect on her. She'd never even tried to crack jokes before she met him.

He shifted his book bag to the other shoulder and leaned one hand against the wall, blocking her path. "I know where you were Saturday night, Heather. You weren't visiting your cousins like you said."

Heather swallowed hard. She was still half asleep. She didn't want a big confrontation with Ben now in the middle of the hall with half of Twin Valley High looking on.

"So that was *you* following us?" she asked, sighing.

"Huh? I didn't follow you," he said angrily. "I didn't have to follow you."

"What do you mean?" Her hands suddenly felt ice-cold. She had a feeling she knew what he was about to say.

"Your uncle told me you had a date with another guy."

"I could *kill* him!" Heather screamed.

Several kids turned to stare at her, surprised expressions on their faces.

She could feel her face turning red. How could her uncle do that to her? *Why* did he do it? Just to embarrass her? Just out of sheer meanness?

"Look, Heather, if you want to go out with some-body else . . . well, I guess there's nothing I can do," Ben said, nervously raking a hand back through his straight black hair, his dark eyes revealing their hurt. "But come on. You didn't have to lie to me, did you?"

"Uncle James had no business telling you," Heather said, unable to control her fury at her uncle.

"That's not the point," Ben insisted angrily, rais-ing his voice so that more heads turned from their lockers to see what the fuss was about. "I don't care about your uncle. I care about you. And you lied to me."

Heather started to say something, she wasn't sure what.

But Ben didn't give her a chance. He made a disgusted face. "We're supposed to trust each other. Not sneak around with other people and tell each other lies." He clomped off down the hall, taking long, angry strides, his work boots thudding loudly against the hard floor.

I didn't want to hurt Ben. I didn't want him to know, Heather thought. It was just one date, after all.

Uncle James is such a meddler. He has no life of

his own, so he's constantly interfering in mine.

I could kill him. I really could.

The bell rang just above her head, startling her. "Hey, Heather," a girl called. "You're going to be late."

Heather didn't see who it was, didn't recognize the voice. She grabbed her book bag off the floor and hurried down the nearly empty hallway. Ben's hurt, angry face, his fiery black eyes, his accusing stare followed her all the way to her seat.

She couldn't concentrate all morning. She found herself daydreaming, thinking of Snowman, of how nice he was and what a good time she'd had with him Saturday night.

He'd turned out to be a much better dancer than he claimed. But of course that wasn't important. What mattered to Heather was that she felt so comfortable with him. It hadn't seemed like a first date at all.

He seemed so understanding. He was such a good listener, and he was really interested in what she had to say. She didn't feel at all shy around him the way she did with other boys, even Ben sometimes.

They danced for hours. Then he drove them to a Chinese restaurant just off the State University campus, where they had egg rolls and wonton soup, and talked comfortably, like old friends, as if they'd known each other for years.

Heather had ended up telling him her whole life story, all about her unhappy life being brought up by her aunt and uncle, about her trust fund and the checking account Uncle James wouldn't let her use, about all the restrictions, all of the rules, all of the problems she had to put up with because of her uncle. She even told him about the fantasies she had, the fantasies of murdering her uncle.

Snowman, it turned out, had a similar unhappy story to tell. His father's death had shocked the family. His mother had to devote all of her time to earning a living, to keeping the family together. She had little time to pay attention to Snowman and his little brother.

Moving to Twin Valley had made their lives even more difficult. His mother was working two jobs, and there still didn't seem to be enough money to pay the bills each month. Snowman had even considered dropping out of school and getting a job to help out. But his mother had convinced him to stay in school. He had only this one last year, after all.

When they kissed good night, Heather reached her arms around him and pulled him close. She already felt close to him. She wanted to feel even closer.

He seemed a little surprised by the power of her emotion. Surprised and pleased. Then she whispered good night and ran into the house.

Later, in bed, Heather drifted into an untroubled sleep and dreamed about snowy mountains. Uncle James didn't appear in her dreams once.

The next morning, while her aunt was in church and her uncle was working on finishing the room over the garage, Heather hurried to the phone in the living room and called Kim to tell her all about her date. Kim listened with a mixture of surprise, delight, and envy, her hoarse, scratchy voice sounding even more comical so early in the morning.

Now, sitting in English composition, not hearing a word Mrs. Leak was saying, Heather couldn't wait for lunch so she could discuss Snowman with Kim even more.

But lunch was a little disappointing. Kim mainly wanted to talk about Ben. He had called her on Sunday to find out what was going on with Heather, who this new guy was. "Your uncle had no right to squeal like that," Kim said heatedly. "Are you going to tell him off or what?"

Heather sighed. "Tell Uncle James off? Are you kidding, Kim? He'd love that. It would give him an excuse to ground me for a month."

"Then what are you going to do? Aren't you even going to tell him to mind his own business, to let you have a little space?"

"No," Heather said, poking at her macaroni and cheese with the bent tines of her fork. "Know what I'm going to do? Nothing. I'm not going to mention it. That's the best way to get back at my uncle. It'll drive him crazy."

"You've got a lot more cool than me," Kim said, biting the crusts off her peanut-butter-and-jelly sandwich.

"I just know Uncle James," Heather said bitterly. "I know his evil mind. I know his stupid power games. When he comes home after work tonight, he'll be dying for me to come yelling and screaming at him about telling Ben about my date."

Heather was right. She knew her uncle very well.

At their solemn dinner table that night, he kept looking at her expectantly, as if waiting for her to say something. But Heather refused to play his game. She talked to her aunt and pretended everything was just fine.

Finally Uncle James couldn't take it anymore. "Are you going to go out with that albino again?" he asked.

"James. Really," Aunt Belle said, shaking her head disapprovingly.

He ignored her and glared at Heather.

"Yeah. I guess," she said, eyes on her plate. "He's not an albino. Could you pass the roast beef, please?"

"He seemed very nice. Very polite," Aunt Belle said, smiling nervously at Heather.

"He makes Ben look almost human," Uncle James said, snickering into his napkin. He turned to his wife. "Pretty fancy dinner." It wasn't a compliment. It was a complaint. "Guess you think we can afford roast beef every night of the week."

"It was on special, James," she said, passing the platter to Heather. "Is it rare enough for you, dear?"

"No. Is it ever?" he grumbled. He swallowed a mouthful of cooked carrots, then turned back to Heather. "You know, it's just as easy to go out with a boy with money as it is with some poor lout."

Heather concentrated on her food and tried to ignore him. She just didn't want to get into a fight with her uncle over Snowman.

"Did you hear me?" he asked, his thin voice rising in pitch.

"Yes," Heather muttered without looking at him.

"Something wrong with that boy. That white hair. It's not right. Must be nutritional or something."

"My cousin Adele had white hair from the time she was twelve," Aunt Belle said thoughtfully.

"Something wrong with her, too," James said, scowling, pushing the boiled potatoes around on his plate.

"Poor Adele," Aunt Belle said mysteriously.

"May I be excused?" Heather asked, and climbed quickly to her feet.

"You haven't finished what's on your plate," Uncle James said, pointing at her plate with his fork.

"I'm not very hungry," she said. She started to walk toward the dining room entranceway.

"I said sit down and finish your plate," he growled.

"I'm sixteen years old," Heather said, feeling herself lose control. "I'm a little too old to be told what to eat and what not to eat."

She hurried toward the door, but her uncle leaped up from his place, stepped away from the table, and grabbed her arm.

"Let go of me!" Heather screamed. She tried to pull out of his grasp.

"James — let her go!" Aunt Belle cried, very alarmed.

"I won't be spoken to like that in my own house!" he bellowed.

In a fury, he jerked her by the arm. She stumbled backward. As she fell, her back hit the corner of the mahogany dining room buffet. She cried out as a sharp, paralyzing stab of pain coursed through her body.

"James — what have you done to her?" Aunt Belle screamed, her open hands pressed against the sides of her face in horror.

Chapter 12

Uncle James apologized grudgingly. Then he accused Heather of spoiling his dinner. Aunt Belle had to lead him to the den, where he collapsed on the couch, complaining of stomach pains, trying to make Heather feel guilty.

Heather threw on her coat and hurried out of the house. Her back still ached as she drove to work. She knew she had a nasty bruise, but she was okay. It was the first time her uncle had ever hurt her physically. It was an accident, she realized, but she couldn't help feeling frightened.

"Why don't you die? Die, die, die." The words repeated in her mind as she pulled into the Twin Valley Mall parking lot.

She wondered if Snowman would show up at the restaurant. She hoped he would.

As she entered the ladies' room to put on her

uniform, she found herself thinking of Ben. What should she do about Ben? She'd never had a problem like this.

She knew she had to apologize. She didn't want Ben to be angry with her. He had acted so furious, so betrayed before school that morning.

And of course he had a right to feel betrayed.

She had to make Ben understand. She had to make him forgive her. She wanted to keep going out with him. He was so nice, so understanding. He knew her so well. And he made her laugh.

She really cared about Ben.

But she also wanted to go out with Snowman again. He seemed so much more exciting to her now.

What to do?

She thought about it all through work. Her mind was half in the restaurant, half in her thoughts, and her eyes were on the doorway, watching for Snowman.

He didn't come in that night.

When Heather got home, she waited for her aunt and uncle to go up to their room. Then she sat down in the living room and called Ben. Her heart was thudding in her chest. She didn't really know what she was going to say.

Ben didn't help make it any easier. He grunted into the phone, responding to her in monosyllabic replies.

She apologized for making up the story about visiting her aunt's cousins. He remained silent. She said she still wanted to go out with him.

"That sounds okay," he said in a flat monotone.

"Can I be really honest with you?" Heather asked, coiling the phone wire nervously around her wrist.

"Uh-oh," was Ben's only reply.

"I want to go out with Snowman, too," she said.

"Who?"

"Another boy."

Silence.

"Come on, Ben," she said finally. "I'm being totally honest with you."

"What am I supposed to say — thank you?" he snapped sarcastically.

"Ben — "

"It's *my* turn to be honest, Heather. Don't call me anymore. Good-bye."

There was a loud click, followed by silence. After a few seconds, the dial tone buzzed in Heather's ear.

She sat in the hard-backed armchair, the receiver in her hand. "You yakking on the phone this late?" Uncle James called down from upstairs, his voice startling her. She dropped the receiver. It fell, pulling the phone to the floor with a loud clatter.

"I was just — "

"Hang it up — unless you want to start paying the phone bills," he said. She heard him muttering under his breath as he padded back to his room.

The next night Snowman came into the restaurant, sliding his long legs under the table of the last booth. Heather finished taking an order and hurried down the row of booths to greet him.

"Hi." She suddenly felt shy.

"How's it going?" he asked, giving her his best crinkly-eyed smile. He wore a black sweatshirt under his oversized overcoat.

"Not too bad tonight. Hold on. I've got to go put this order in." She tore the sheet off the pad and handed it through the kitchen window to Mel. Then she brought Snowman a hamburger and a Coke.

"Thanks." He began to eat hungrily.

"I looked for you in school yesterday morning," Heather said, watching the kitchen window.

"Oh, yeah?" He didn't look up from his hamburger.

"I went to your homeroom, but you weren't there."

"I know. I . . . uh . . . had to stay home yesterday morning. Some . . . family things."

"Oh. Is everything okay?" Heather asked with real concern.

Snowman just shrugged. His face didn't reveal any emotion. He brushed back his white hair. His dark eyes reflected the fluorescent ceiling lights.

"I asked this girl I know. She said you weren't in Louper's homeroom," Heather said, her eyes on the lookout for Mel.

"Yeah. I know. Do you think I could have some fries? I'm really starving."

"Sure. I guess. Wait till Mel gets away from the

french fry machine. I'll get you a plate. You didn't have dinner?"

"No. Mom had to work late and . . . they moved me."

"What?"

"They moved me out of that homeroom." He pulled several paper napkins out of the dispenser and wiped ketchup from his cheek. "That's why they didn't know me there. Like you said, it was a sophomore homeroom. It was a mix-up. I'm not used to such a big school, you know. You can get lost in that place." He grinned up at her.

"Well, whose homeroom are you in now?" Heather asked.

He started to answer her, but she heard Mel hitting the bell indicating that somebody's food was ready, and she hurried to pick it up. Things got busy, as they usually did right before closing, and Heather didn't have a chance to talk to Snowman anymore.

Just before nine she looked over to see him give her a wave, mouthing the words "Thank you," and he walked out, his hands stuffed into the pockets of the long, fifties-style overcoat.

Cleaning up his table, she found another folded-up piece of paper. This one had a little snowman drawn on it and the words *Meet Me at Swan Park, Saturday Afternoon.*

A short while later she had changed into her street clothes, said good night to Marjorie and Mel, and headed across the vast, nearly empty parking lot to her car. It was a cold, moonless night. A strong, gusting wind had come down from the north, blowing sheets of powdery, loose snow across the lot.

Heather ducked her head and jogged against the driving wind to her car. It took four tries to start it up. Uncle James had refused to give it a winter tune-up, saying that he couldn't afford it. The car had been protesting its ill treatment all winter.

Finally Heather pulled out onto Valley Drive, her headlights piercing the darkness and the blowing snow. She had gone about six blocks when she noticed the car following closely behind her.

It was a Taurus. A black Ford Taurus. Or maybe it just looked black because it was so dark on Valley Drive. Heather couldn't see the driver.

I wish this clown wouldn't ride right on my tail, she thought. Especially since there are still so many slippery patches on the road.

When she turned onto Century, she was surprised to see that the Taurus turned with her.

Is it following me? That was her first thought.

Doesn't Ben's mother drive a Taurus? That was her second thought.

Century was a wide avenue. Heather slowed down, pulling far to the right, and gave the Taurus a chance to pass.

But the Taurus slowed down, too. It didn't pass.

Someone is following me, she thought, a feeling of dread making her shiver.

Now I'm acting crazy, just like Snowman.

She turned right at the next intersection. She wasn't sure what street it was. She just wanted to see if the car would follow.

Yes.

The black Taurus kept close behind her.

Well, whoever it is, isn't being very subtle about it, Heather thought. When people follow a car in the movies, they stay far enough back so the person doesn't become suspicious.

It's got to be an amateur.

It's *got* to be Ben.

No, it *can't* be Ben.

Ben wouldn't pull a childish stunt like this — would he?

She was safe in the car. Why did she feel so frightened?

Because whoever it was, was *trying* to frighten her.

Well, there's one way to prove if it's Ben or not, she thought, stepping on the gas. She was only a few blocks from his house. She'd drive there and see.

Staring into the rearview mirror, she struggled to make out the face of the driver as she bolted through a four-way stop and roared onto Ben's block. But the windshield of the car behind was covered in shadow as if a dark curtain had been pulled over it.

She couldn't even see if the car *had* a driver!

Ben's house was three houses away on the left. She slowed as his driveway came into view.

Was his mother's black Taurus in the drive?

A yellow light over the garage door threw a wide cone of light over the driveway.

The Taurus wasn't there.

The driveway was empty.

"Wow."

Heather spun the wheel sharply to the left and pulled into the drive.

The driver of the black Taurus must have been surprised by Heather's move. The Taurus's tires squealed and skidded over the pavement.

Heather pulled her car to a stop halfway up the drive.

She pushed open the car door and turned toward the street, trying to get a good look at the black Taurus. But with a roar of acceleration it sped away. The driver was a blur, surrounded by darkness.

Heather climbed out of the car, breathing hard.

She realized she was shaking all over.

Maybe it was just some high school kid clowning around, she thought, trying to calm herself down.

Or just some creep who got his kicks by scaring people at night.

Or was it Ben?

Her breath rose up in small puffs of white steam. She half walked, half ran up the flagstone walk to the front door and rang the bell.

Are you home, Ben?

Or was that you in the car?

Silence.

She rang the bell again.

She backed up a few steps to look in the living room window. The house was completely dark. The porch light and the light over the garage were the only lights on.

No one was home.

Chapter 13

It had snowed all of Friday night, a fresh white covering for the graying snow already on the ground. Heather parked the car at the curb and crossed the street to the park, her boots sinking in over her ankles, making a pleasant crunching sound with each step.

The air smelled clean and crisp and piney. Someone must have had a wood fire burning nearby. Heather inhaled the sweet, tangy aroma and smiled.

Swan Park began on a gently sloping hill, which leveled into a wide, sweeping plateau with woods on the left and a small, oval-shaped lake on the right. Six or eight swans lived on the lake in the summer, which may have been the reason behind the park's name. The swans weren't there in the wintertime. Heather had always wondered where they went.

She started up the low hill, which seemed much steeper because of the deep, slippery snow. There was no wind at all. Nothing moved. Heather suddenly felt as if she were in a painting of some kind, a painting of white on white, everything clean and pure, and unreal.

"Hey — Heather!"

She looked up to see Snowman waving to her from the top of the hill. "Come on up. Isn't this great?" he called, kicking at the snow.

He looks like a long, skinny colt, she thought. A colt with a long mane of white hair.

She started to jog up the hill, slipping and sliding, but making steady progress. He took both her hands when she neared the top and pulled her the rest of the way, both of them slipping in a drift that came up to the top of their boots.

"So much snow," he said as Heather struggled to catch her breath. "I'm just glad of one thing."

"What's that?"

"Glad I don't have to shovel it!"

They both laughed. His dark eyes sparkled like black coals against the bright white surroundings.

Like snowman eyes, she thought.

"Hey, this was a great idea," she said, her gloved hands still in his.

"What was?"

"Coming here today. I would've just stayed home and moped around the house."

He let go of her hands and started walking toward the woods, the dark trees all bare except for the covering of snow on their branches. Heather looked back to the lake. Several kids were having a snowball fight near the shore. Behind them, about a dozen people in bright reds and blues were ice-skating on the frozen lake.

"It looks like a postcard or something," Heather said. "It's too bright and corny to be true."

"Maybe it isn't true," Snowman said mysteriously, and kept leading the way to the woods.

"What's that supposed to mean?" she asked, puzzled, hurrying to catch up with him.

He didn't reply.

"Hey, let's build a snowman," she said, clapping her gloves together, watching her white, steamy breath sail up against the blue sky. "I haven't built a snowman since I was a kid."

"Okay. Great idea," he said, grinning back at her.

"I remember once I built a snowman in the front yard and put one of Uncle James's old hats on it. When he came home, he was furious. He punished me for ruining his hat. Can you believe that? And I knew he hadn't worn the hat in years."

"He's a bad dude," Snowman said, shaking his head. He had a long red wool scarf wrapped around his neck outside his overcoat.

"Where are we going?" Heather asked, realizing they were entering the woods.

"Just keep going," he said, ducking his head to avoid walking into a low tree branch.

"But we can't build a snowman in the woods," she protested. "Come on — turn around. Let's build it down there, closer to the lake."

"I know a secret place," he said quietly.

Their boots crunched over sticks and dried weeds buried under the snow. Somewhere nearby a woodpecker tapped out a message high on a tree trunk.

"A secret place? You just moved here," Heather said, stepping over a fallen log, trying to keep up with him. "How can you know a secret place?"

He laughed. "I have my ways," he said in a funny foreign accent.

"But these woods go on forever," Heather protested.

"That's what I like about you. You're so trusting. Just chill out for a minute. We're almost there."

Heather turned to look back as she continued walking. She couldn't see the lake anymore. They were too far into the woods. Surrounded by barren, snow-covered trees, their limbs reaching out like arms to encircle her.

She had a sudden tremor of doubt.

Maybe this isn't such a smart thing. Going deep into these woods, far from everyone else, with this . . . stranger.

But then she scolded herself for even momentarily thinking such a thing about Snowman.

That's what you've done to me, Uncle James, she thought. You've made me suspicious of everyone.

"Oh!"

A chipmunk scampered right past her feet and disappeared into a hollow tree trunk. "Did you see that? A chipmunk!" she exclaimed.

Snowman was several yards ahead of her, making a twisting path through the thick bushes and tall weeds. She walked in his footprints, keeping one eye on the ground, one eye on him.

"Almost there," he repeated quietly.

"You sound like my dentist," she said. " 'Almost done. We're almost done.' And then he goes on drilling for another twenty minutes."

But then, suddenly, there they were.

To Heather's surprise, the trees suddenly ended and they stepped out into a small, circular, flat clearing.

"Oh! It's so pretty!" she exclaimed, standing in the center of it and twirling around, making the trees seem to whirl by. "How did you ever find this place? It's so totally secluded."

He just smiled.

"I thought it was a neat place," he said, retying the red scarf. "Come on. Let's build a really big snowman."

They started with a small snowball. Heather rolled it until it was a little larger, and then a little larger, and then a little larger. Now it was big enough for both of them to roll together.

"It's great packing snow," Snowman said, bumping into her as he tried to roll the big snowball. "Just wet enough."

"Is this the head or the body?" she asked.

"Let's try to do one with three parts. You know — a head and *two* body sections," he said excitedly. "Like in the cartoons."

"I feel like I'm in a cartoon or something," Heather said, pushing too hard and sliding right off the ball, face down into the snow.

"Now you *look* like you're in a cartoon," Snowman said. "How'd you do that?"

"Just naturally graceful," she said, pulling herself up. He came over and helped brush the snow off the front of her down jacket.

She thought maybe he was going to kiss her. But he returned to the snowball instead.

"Hey — "

She looked past him to the woods. What was that?

Someone behind that tree.

Yes.

Someone was there. Someone was hiding behind that wide-trunked tree, spying on them.

"Hey, Snowman — " she called softly.

He didn't hear her.

She looked back into the woods. No one there now.

Whoever it was had left.

She listened. She couldn't hear any footsteps. No boots walking over the crackling sticks and weeds.

She stared into the trees.

No one. Nothing moved.

I imagined it, she told herself. Of all the crazy things. Who would be way up here in the woods? No one even knows this little clearing exists.

She suddenly remembered the black Taurus that

had followed her. Was this the same person?

No. Stop it. Don't make yourself crazy.

There's no one there.

She put it out of her mind and started a new snowball. "This'll be the head," she said.

"Too bad you didn't bring one of your uncle's hats," Snowman joked.

The afternoon sun was lowering behind the trees when they got the Snowman finished. The air was picking up a wet, heavy chill.

But Heather felt warm from her hard work. In fact, she was perspiring.

"It's real cute," she said, stepping back to admire their handiwork.

"A masterpiece," he said, standing very close to her.

"Well, let's not go too far," she said.

"It's a little lumpy," he admitted.

"But I like it anyway," she said turning to him.

And as soon as she did, he wrapped his arms around her, and lowered his face to hers and kissed her, softly at first, and then hungrily.

She kissed him back, wrapping her arms around the back of his overcoat, holding onto him tightly.

I don't want this afternoon to end, she thought, closing her eyes as if making a wish.

This was the nicest afternoon of my life.

Please, please, don't let it end.

But when she opened her eyes, Snowman pulled his face away, keeping his arms around her. "I like you," he said. "A lot."

"I like you, too," she said, feeling awkward but meaning it.

"This is our special place," he said softly. "It's our special snowman and our special place. No one knows it's here but us."

She pulled his head down and kissed him again.

"We'd better head back. It's getting dark," she said finally. "I had a great afternoon, Snowman."

"Me, too," he said, his dark eyes burning into hers.

"Come on. You've got to lead the way out of these woods," she said, looking up at the darkening sky.

"Okay. No problem," he said.

But instead of starting toward the road, he walked over to the snowman in the middle of the clearing. He turned and quickly drove his elbow into the snowman's head. The head toppled off the round, white body and fell onto the snow with a quiet plop.

Then, without uttering a word, Snowman turned back and started into the woods.

"Hey — why'd you do that?" Heather asked, hurrying after him.

He turned back to her, shrugged his shoulders, and flashed her his boyish grin.

Chapter 14

"What's for dinner?" Uncle James called from his armchair in the living room.

"Chicken," Aunt Belle answered, her voice wafting in with the good smells from the kitchen.

"Well, you'd better just serve white meat if that albino is coming to dinner!" He slapped his knees and laughed his high, girlish laugh at his own joke.

"Uncle James, that isn't funny," Heather said softly. "Why are you trying to make me mad?"

He pulled his newspaper down below his chin and looked at her through his thick reading glasses. "Hey, get a sense of humor," he said dryly. He pulled the newspaper back up over his face. "Whatever happened to that *old* boyfriend of yours?"

"You mean Ben?" Heather didn't want to discuss Ben with her uncle. Why was he forcing her to? Just to make her uncomfortable, of course.

"Ben," he muttered from behind his paper. "Nice

guy. Don't know *what* he saw in you!" He snickered loudly.

I knew that inviting Snowman to dinner was a dreadful mistake, Heather thought glumly. She sat staring at the phone, wishing it would ring, wishing it would be Snowman saying he couldn't make it after all.

Actually, it had been Snowman's idea. It was the *last* thing Heather would ever suggest! She wouldn't wish Uncle James on her worst enemy.

But Snowman had insisted. It was last Wednesday night. They were in her car in the mall parking lot. It was late. The restaurant had just closed. There were no other cars around. She was telling him about her uncle's new car.

"Where'd he get the bread to buy a new Volvo station wagon?" Snowman had exclaimed, his arm cozily around her shoulders.

"That's what *I* want to know," Heather had replied bitterly.

"He's always talking about how poor he is, right? How you're going to have to start chipping in on the food bills?" Snowman already knew many of her complaints about her uncle.

"I think he's using my money," Heather said. "From my trust fund."

"You mean he's stealing it?"

"Yeah. I think so. But there's no way I can prove it."

"You need to get a lawyer," Snowman said heatedly. "Someone you can trust. You can't let your uncle — "

"Oh, let's stop talking about him," Heather cried, and buried her face against Snowman's shoulder.

"How come you never invite me over?" he asked suddenly, lowering his voice.

The question took her by surprise. She sat up. "Huh? You mean, like, for dinner or something?"

"Yeah."

"You're serious?"

"Sure."

"But why would you want to have dinner with Uncle James? You like being picked apart while you eat? You like being insulted and teased?"

He laughed. "Yeah. I thrive on it."

"You're weird."

"I can handle your uncle," he said, staring straight ahead.

"Would you like to make a little bet?" Heather asked playfully.

"A bet? Sure. What kind of bet?"

"I'll bet you that you can't last an entire dinner with him."

"What do you mean, Heather?"

"That you'll run screaming from the house before dinner is over." She laughed even though she was being serious.

"Maybe your uncle will run screaming from the house," Snowman said, grinning at her. "*I have ways to deal with uncles*," he said in that funny foreign accent he sometimes dropped into.

"He'll probably toss you out on your butt," she said. "Once he chased Ben all the way down the driveway. And he kind of *liked* Ben!"

Ben.

She hadn't thought about Ben in days.

Thinking about him now gave her a sudden pang, a heavy feeling in her chest.

She realized she missed Ben.

She had tried to call him once, but after a whispered conversation on the other end of the line, his mother said he wasn't there. And whenever Heather approached him in school, he deliberately turned and walked away from her.

Ben.

Should she try to call him again? Should she send him a note? That might be best. But what could she say? That she missed him? That she wanted to keep him as a friend?

That sounded so corny, so disgusting.

"So are you going to invite me to dinner or not?" Snowman's low voice interrupted her thoughts.

"Okay. If you insist. You're invited. Come next Wednesday night. Don't come too late, though. Uncle James gets real testy if he doesn't eat promptly at six-thirty."

"Is your aunt a good cook?"

"Not especially."

"No? How come?"

"She's too nervous to be a good cook."

"Wow. You do make this invitation sound real . . . inviting!"

"It was *your* idea," she reminded him. "And don't forget our bet."

"Okay. Fine." He leaned close to her. "What are we betting?" He didn't wait for a reply. "I know! How about we bet a kiss?"

As he kissed her, she wondered how her uncle was going to react to having Snowman at the dinner table.

He'll find some way to cause a scene. He'll find some way to humiliate me, she thought. He always does.

She tried to push her uncle out of her mind as she held Snowman close.

"Please pass the rice to Bill," Aunt Belle said to Heather. The smile on her face indicated her pleasure at seeing Snowman wolf down her food so vigorously.

Heather was always surprised by the way Snowman ate. He was usually controlled, almost careful. But whenever he ate, he shoveled the food into his mouth as if he hadn't eaten in days.

Heather knew that Snowman didn't have much money. Maybe he really doesn't get to eat regularly, she thought.

Snowman took the bowl of rice and spooned a third big helping onto his plate. "Everything's really good, Mrs. Dickson," he said, giving her a warm, appreciative smile and then digging into the steaming, white rice.

Much to Heather's relief, Uncle James had been pretty quiet up to this point. But now, his plate nearly empty, he cleared his throat and stared at Snowman disapprovingly, watching him hungrily gulp down the rice.

"Guess they don't feed you too well at home?" Uncle James said with a sneer.

Snowman pretended Heather's uncle had made a joke, and laughed politely.

"Belle, maybe you'd better give the boy a doggie bag for later," Uncle James said, and cleared his throat loudly again.

"It's all so delicious. I don't get much home-cooked food," Snowman said.

"What does your mother do?" Uncle James asked, making the question sound like an accusation.

"Well, she's a nurse."

"And that gives her an excuse not to put dinner on the table?" Uncle James asked, his voice rising, starting to sound agitated.

Oh, no. Here we go, thought Heather. He's going to launch into one of his sexist speeches about how it's a woman's job to make sure dinner is on the table promptly every night.

A feeling of dread made her food sit heavily in her stomach. Heather wished she and Snowman could just excuse themselves and get away now, before Uncle James got started.

"Well, she works very long shifts," Snowman said, swallowing a piece of chicken. "And my little brother isn't well, so — "

"And where's your father?" Uncle James asked, scratching the back of his scalp.

"He *told* you," Heather broke in, not meaning to sound so shrill. "He's dead."

"Oh. Right. Sorry," her uncle said, not sounding the least bit sorry. "Well, what did he do when he was alive?"

"Uncle James — please!" Heather cried. She looked to her aunt, as if saying, "Please stop him," but Aunt Belle just shrugged.

"He was a salesman," Snowman said, finishing his string beans.

"Don't eat the coating off the plate," Uncle James said, watching Snowman chew. Snowman laughed again, as if Uncle James had cracked a funny joke.

Uncle James proceeded to ask a string of questions about Snowman's family and background. Snowman answered calmly and politely, but Heather thought she would burst from anger. What right did her uncle have to sit there and give Snowman the third degree? Didn't he realize what a nasty, old busybody he sounded like?

Heather was totally embarrassed, but somehow she managed to hold herself in.

She faded out of the conversation. No one was talking to her, anyway. Her mind wandered. Her uncle's shrill voice continued in the background, punctuated by Snowman's short answers.

Poor Snowman, she thought. He'll be answering my uncle's questions until his hair turns white! She giggled. She hadn't meant to make a joke.

No one paid any attention to her. When her aunt got up to clear the table, Heather started to follow. "No. No. Sit," her aunt said. "Talk with your friend."

Why won't you let me escape from this? Heather thought. Her aunt squeezed her shoulder gently, as if to say, "Just stay calm. Your uncle will quit soon."

But he continued his barrage of questions through the apple pie and coffee. Snowman kept shooting glances at Heather. She kept trying to interrupt her uncle, but he ignored her as usual.

"Well, Burt," Uncle James said, scraping the pie crumbs on his plate with his dessert fork.

"It's *Bill*," Heather interrupted.

"Whatever," her uncle said, frowning. "I hope you don't get any ideas about Heather."

"What?!" Heather cried, feeling her face grow hot.

"I know what you're up to with her," Uncle James said, pressing his thin lips together in an expression of disapproval.

"James — I think — " Aunt Belle finally stepped in. But Uncle James held up his hand to silence her.

"Well, go ahead. Have a good time," Uncle James continued, his watery eyes behind his thick glasses staring into Snowman's. "But just don't get any serious ideas about her."

"Now, just a minute — " Snowman, looking very

uncomfortable, pushed back his chair.

"Uncle James — enough!" Heather cried.

"Because Heather is going to come into a great deal of money someday," Uncle James said, ignoring them both, unwilling to stop until he had finished his complete speech. "And believe me, Burt, or Bill, or whatever your name is, she's going to end up with someone from her own class. Not some white-haired freak whose mother can't even put dinner on the table."

Heather sat. Stunned.

Aunt Belle leaned forward, her mouth wide open, staring at her husband in shock at his rudeness.

Looking very tense and pale, his eyes narrowed in anger, Snowman jumped to his feet.

Uncle James stood up quickly, as if accepting a challenge.

Heather's heart began to pound. Snowman and her uncle stood only a few feet apart, glaring angrily at each other.

Neither of them said a word.

What's going to happen now? Heather wondered.

Is there going to be a fight?

Chapter 15

Snowman's face turned to ice.

All expression drained from his face. He suddenly looked to Heather like a department store mannequin.

He pushed his chair back in. It scraped loudly against the hardwood floor.

Heather's uncle didn't move. He kept his eyes trained on Snowman, as if waiting for him to make a move, to challenge him in some way.

Uncle James is actually gloating, Heather thought angrily. He's enjoying this. He did this deliberately. He had planned it all along.

Snowman turned away from her uncle and, his face still expressionless, his hands gripping the chairback tightly, thanked Heather's aunt. "It was a great dinner. Thanks," he said, his voice calm, smooth, revealing no nervousness or tension.

"Talk to you later, Heather," he said, and turned quickly, giving Uncle James his back, and walked toward the front door taking long, steady strides.

"Snowman, wait — " Heather shouted.

The front door slammed.

"What's his problem?" Uncle James asked, rolling his eyes in mock innocence.

"I hate you! I really hate you!" Heather screamed. She knocked over her chair as she started to run after Snowman. She heard it clatter to the floor, heard her uncle swear loudly, heard Aunt Belle calling after her.

But she grabbed her down jacket from the front closet, pulled open the door, and ran out into the snow after Snowman. He was walking quickly, his boots crunching over the hard snow, probably heading to the bus stop three corners down on Brock Street.

He had the collar of his overcoat turned up. His head was hunched down so that all Heather could see was his long, white hair over the coat collar, reflected in the blue-white light of the street lamps.

"Snowman — wait!"

He kept walking. Didn't he hear her?

Or was he so angry, he didn't want to stop for her?

She ran, slipping in her sneakers. She fell once, picked herself up, and continued after him. "Snowman — wait up!"

He heard her this time. He spun around, surprised.

He looked so pale under the streetlight. Ghostly pale.

He smiled.

She caught up to him, breathing hard, gasping, her jacket open, icy-cold water already starting to soak through her sneakers.

"I guess you win the bet," he said, his dark eyes catching the light of the street lamp.

He didn't seem at all upset.

"I could kill him," Heather said heatedly. "Really. I could *kill* him!"

He didn't reply. He reached forward and put his hands on her shoulders. "No problem," he said, whispering suddenly. "Really."

"But he insulted you!" Heather cried, not understanding how Snowman could be so calm and accepting over what had just happened. "He deliberately insulted you — and embarrassed me. He's such a pig! He's such a dirty, stinking — "

He playfully put a hand over her mouth to stop her. His hand felt hot against her face despite the cold of the night.

"Sshhhh. It's no problem. Really."

Heather pulled out of his grasp. "How can you *say* that? How can you stay so calm after he — after he — "

Snowman shrugged. "It was just words."

"Just *words*?!" She was shrieking, her voice so high she didn't recognize it. But she didn't care. This was the worst thing her uncle had ever done to her.

"Heather, listen — "

Snowman looked so pale in the dim light.

She started to shiver. Was it from the cold, or because she was so upset?

"He doesn't care what he says," Heather cried. "He thinks he can say anything, *do* anything. He thinks he can embarrass me, humiliate me in front of anyone. I — I — "

"It's just words," Snowman repeated. He tried to zip her jacket for her, but he couldn't get the zipper started.

Something about the way he was struggling so intently made her start to forget how angry she was. She reached down and covered Snowman's hands with hers. Then she brushed his hands away and zipped the jacket. It's cold," she said, watching her steamy breath trail up to the black sky.

"You shouldn't let your uncle get to you," Snowman said, starting to walk toward the bus stop.

Heather hurried to catch up to him, and took his arm. "He treats me like I'm a speck of dirt. Just the way he treated you. How can you be so calm about it? How can you stand to have him sit there and say such horrible things to you?"

"I've got other problems," Snowman said quietly, leaning into the wind, staring straight ahead. His big overcoat flapped noisily in the sudden gusts.

Heather held on tightly to his arm as they continued to walk. "What?"

"I've got other problems. More serious than your

uncle." For the first time, he showed a little emotion.

Heather stopped walking, forcing him to stop. "What? What's the matter?"

He seemed reluctant to tell her. "It's not your problem, really."

"Tell me. Please. What's the matter, Snowman?"

"It's my brother." His voice cracked. "He's pretty sick. He needs an operation."

"What's wrong with him?"

"I — I really don't understand it. Something about his kidneys. It's pretty bad. He has to have this operation. And we — well . . . we can't afford it."

"But you said your mom's a nurse. Wouldn't the hospital she works for — ?"

"She doesn't work for a hospital," Snowman interrupted. He bent down, scooped up some snow in his bare hand, and formed it into a tight snowball. "She's a private nurse. She cares for some old lady in her apartment."

"Oh. I see." Heather didn't know what to say.

Snowman reared his arm back and heaved the snowball at a car three quarters of the way down the block. It hit the back window with a loud *splat*.

"I'm going to get a job," he said.

"An after-school job?"

"Maybe a full-time job. I don't know."

"You mean drop out of school?"

"Yeah. Just until I make enough money to . . . to . . ." He looked away. He was embarrassed to be showing so much emotion. "I don't know what to do, really. Even if I get a job, I wouldn't have the money in time to pay for Eddie's operation. It — it's two thousand dollars."

"Well, maybe . . ."

"Mom tried to get a loan, but the bank turned her down. They said she had no collateral, that her job was only a temporary one."

They trudged through the snow in silence for a few moments. Somewhere from several blocks away the sound of a police siren cut through the frozen night air.

Suddenly Heather had an idea. She squeezed Snowman's arm.

"Ow."

"Sorry. Didn't mean to squeeze so hard. Listen. I can lend you the money."

His dark eyes opened wide with surprise. "Huh?"

"You heard me. I can lend you the two thousand dollars. I have it in my checking account, the one Uncle James actually lets me keep."

"No, Heather." For the first time since she'd known him, he looked genuinely embarrassed.

"I have the money. I could write you a check. You could pay me back whenever. You know. A little at a time after you got your job."

"Heather — stop." He put both hands on her shoulders and drew his face close to hers. His breath smelled of apples. "No. I couldn't."

"But your brother — he has to have the operation right away?"

"The sooner the better," Snowman said grimly, biting his lower lip.

"So okay. Let me write you a check," Heather said. "I have the money. It's just sitting there. This way it'll be put to good use."

A car turned the corner, its tires sliding on a patch of ice. The headlights caught them both by surprise.

Heather raised her arm to shield her eyes. Too late. The whole world seemed to flash bright silver. After the car had passed, the driver swerving wide to move past them, the light stayed in Heather's eyes, making everything looked pink and too bright, as if they were suddenly in a different world or a science-fiction movie set.

"Listen, I've got to go," Snowman said, looking very troubled.

"Where? I'll come with you," Heather said. She really didn't want to have to go back home and confront her uncle.

"No. I — I'd like to be alone for a bit. You know. Try to think things through."

"But — what about the money?"

"No. I couldn't, Heather. Thanks. That's the nicest thing anyone ever offered me. But I just couldn't."

He leaned forward and gave her a quick kiss on the cheek. His lips felt very warm against her skin. Then he turned and started jogging down the snow-covered sidewalk, the oversized raincoat flapping behind him as he moved.

Heather stood watching him, shivering, her hands shoved into her jeans pockets. Why is he being so stubborn about taking the money? she wondered.

Halfway down the block, he turned and cupped his hands to his mouth as a megaphone. "I almost forgot. Thanks for dinner!"

"So you're not speaking to your uncle?"

"No. We haven't said a word to each other ever since that dinner last week. I feel bad for my aunt, though. All the tension in the house makes her even more nervous than usual."

Heather turned away from Kim to see Mel staring at her from the kitchen. "Better order something, Kim," she said. "Otherwise I'm not supposed to be talking to you."

"I'll have a Diet Coke," Kim said, dropping down into the back booth. "When are you going to quit this disgusting job, anyway?"

"Oh, I don't know," Heather said, writing down the Diet Coke on her pad. "It's not such a bad job if you have to have a job."

"Which you don't," Kim said.

"And I met Snowman here. So how bad can it be?"

"Have you seen him since the fabulous dinner?" Kim pulled several napkins out of the dispenser on the table and spit out her gum into them.

"No. I'm really worried. He's got some family problems and — "

Heather looked up to see Snowman pushing open the door of the coffee shop. He was wearing the oversized overcoat, the collar pulled up. His hair was windblown, scattered like a white dandelion head, his face red from the cold.

Kim followed Heather's stare. "Hey, that's him, right?"

Heather nodded.

"I'll finally get to meet the fabulous Snowman."

He came walking up to the booth, a serious expression on his face. "Hi," he said to Heather.

"I'm Heather's best friend, Kim," Kim said before Heather had a chance to say anything.

Snowman glanced down at her, a bit startled. "Hi," he said. "Heather's told me about you."

"You, too," Kim said. "You really do have white hair."

"Yeah, I do." He touched it, as if making sure it was still there. He turned to Heather. "Can I talk to you?"

"Sure. It's almost quitting time." She looked up at the clock. Twenty minutes to go. "Why don't you meet me?"

"Yeah. Okay. Where are you parked?"

He seemed jumpy, impatient. Not his usual cool self.

"By the movie theater," Heather said, looking past him to the kitchen where Mel was busily scraping some eggs off the grill.

"Okay," he said. Then, "Nice to meet you," to Kim, and he hurried out, nearly colliding with Marjorie, who was carrying a tray full of dirty dishes.

"He looked kind of upset," Kim said.

Heather started to reply, her eyes still on the door that Snowman had just exited. But Mel rang the kitchen bell, two rings for Heather, and she hurried to pick up the waiting food.

Snowman *did* look kind of upset, she thought, especially for him. His face usually revealed no emotion at all, even when he was really happy.

But he was definitely not happy tonight.

Luckily the restaurant wasn't very crowded. The rest of the shift went quickly. Kim slurped down her Diet Coke and waved good-bye. Mel was scraping the grease off the grill as Heather wiped the last booth table clean. Then she quickly changed into her street clothes, said good night, and hurried out to the parking lot to meet Snowman.

She found him standing by the car, his hands in his coat pockets. "Oh, I'm sorry. I forgot I locked it," she apologized, fumbling in her bag for the car key.

"That's okay," he said quietly. "It's not that cold." He climbed into the passenger seat, and she jogged around the car to get in on the driver's side.

"Want to drive around a bit? I'll put the heater on, and you can warm up."

"No. I want to talk first," he said, turning his back to the door so that he could face her.

"Sure. What's the matter? I haven't seen you since last week."

"It — it's Eddie," he said.

A large car pulled up to them, its brights on, the headlights invading their privacy, filling the car with bright yellow light.

Snowman grabbed for the door handle, looking very frightened. He started to push open the door, but the car backed up and headed the other way.

"Snowman, it was just turning around," Heather said, startled by how frightened he looked. "Are you okay?"

He closed the car door, his face still filled with fear. "It scared me, that's all," he said, his voice shaky. "Sorry. I'm really jumpy these days. It's not like me, I know."

"Your brother is bad?" Heather asked, putting a hand tenderly on the shoulder of his overcoat, trying to calm him.

"Yeah," Snowman said, raking a hand back through his hair, then scratching his cheek. "He's got to have the operation right away. The doctors say he can't wait any longer."

"Oh, I'm sorry," Heather said. "So will you — "

"Just let me get this out, okay?" he said. "It isn't easy for me. I've sort of been going over it in my mind and — "

"You don't have to be nervous to tell me anything," Heather said, seeing how uncomfortable he was, trying to be helpful.

"Well, the other night, remember, you offered to write me a check. For the two thousand dollars Mom and I need. If you could . . . I mean, I'd really appreciate it if . . ."

"Snowman, I told you, I'd be happy to give you a check. It's no problem. Really."

"I didn't want to," he said, finally looking at her. "I hate asking anyone for money. Especially you. But it's for Eddie. If you could, Heather, I'd really — "

"I have my checkbook right here in my bag," Heather said, pulling open the bag and rummaging inside it.

He turned and looked out his window, obviously embarrassed. "Heather, I — "

"It's no problem. Believe me," she said, turning on the interior light so she could write the check. "The money is just sitting there. I'm so glad it can be put to good use."

He turned back and watched her start to fill out the check, but he didn't say anything. She leaned forward, resting the checkbook on the dashboard to write.

"How should I make it out?"

"To me, I guess. Bill Jeffers."

"Okay. Here it is." She signed her name and carefully tore the check out of the book.

He took it from her and stuffed it quickly, without looking at it, into his overcoat pocket.

"Thanks, Heather. I'll pay you back. Really. I'll pay you back real soon."

Chapter 16

A few evenings later, Heather stepped out the door
of her house after an unpleasantly silent dinner and
was startled to find Ben walking up the driveway.

"Hey — what are *you* doing here?"

He grinned at her nervously. "Wow, I didn't expect such a friendly greeting. I'm overwhelmed."

She laughed and realized she was glad to see him.
"How's it going?" she asked, trying to sound casual.

"Okay." He was wearing a hooded gray sweatshirt under a bulky ski sweater, dark blue corduroys, and a beat-up pair of work boots.

They stood staring at each other awkwardly, a
few yards apart in her driveway. He tried to jam
his hands in his pocket, then crossed his arms in
front of his chest. "I . . . well . . . I kind of miss
you," he said, blushing a little.

"You always were so eloquent," she cracked.

She hadn't talked to him in weeks. But it was so easy to fall back into the old patterns, the same old teasing, the same easy friendship.

He took a few reluctant steps toward her.

"I've missed you, too," she said softly.

It was a warm night, almost balmy. The driveway was puddled with melting snow. The evening air smelled wet and sweet.

"Can we go somewhere and talk?" Ben asked, looking toward her car, which was parked in the street.

"No. I've got to get to the restaurant. I'm already late," Heather said, struggling to read her watch in the gray evening light. "Can I drop you somewhere?"

"Are you still dating that guy?"

The question surprised her. He said it with such suddenness, speaking quickly, as if the question were all one word. She realized that the reason he had come was to ask that question.

"Yeah," she said, kicking at a low mound of wet snow.

She thought about Snowman, pictured him at her dinner table, standing up to Uncle James, pictured him standing in the mall parking lot in that overcoat he seemed to always wear, the red wool scarf tied loosely around him, the collar pulled up to his white hair.

She realized she hadn't seen him since the night she had written the check. She had tried to phone him, eager to find out how his brother was doing. But Information had no listing for a Jeffers in Twin Valley.

She couldn't believe she hadn't asked him for his phone number. She was dying to know if Eddie was okay, how Snowman was doing.

"Then I guess there's no point in us talking," Ben said dejectedly, breaking into her thoughts.

"No. I mean yes," she said, suddenly flustered. "How about Saturday afternoon or something? I — I'd still like to be friends with you." The words felt sticky in her mouth.

Did I *really* just say that? Heather thought.

Ben made a face, as if reading her thoughts.

"Yeah. Well. Maybe."

"Ben, I'm really sorry. I — "

"Later," he said. "You'd better go. Those grease-burgers are piling up." He headed down the driveway, his old work boots sloshing noisily in the wet snow.

She watched him, feeling bad that she had hurt him. He was really a good guy.

Halfway down the drive, he turned back. "How's your uncle?" he shouted.

"The same," she yelled back. "Why?"

"Just wondered," he called. "See you." And he hurried off into the gray evening, disappearing around the tall hedges down by the street.

As she scurried from booth to booth, Heather kept an eye on the door, watching for Snowman, hoping he'd come to see her, desperate to talk with him.

And I've *got* to remember to get his phone number, she told herself.

This is so weird, she thought, realizing how little she knew about him. I don't know his phone number or his address. He's never talked about where he lives. He always comes to the restaurant or to my house.

She realized she hadn't ever seen him in school, either.

But that was probably because he had been staying home much of the time to take care of Eddie.

Why don't I know more about him? she asked, scolding herself. Is it because I'm so self-obsessed? Only concerned about my own problems? Too busy to find out about a boy I really care about?

The next time I see him, I'll ask him a million questions, she told herself.

The next time I see him . . .

"Miss, that's my order up there. It's been ready for ten minutes," an elderly lady sitting alone in the biggest booth called.

"Oh. Sorry." Heather hurried to pick up her BLT.

"What's it like to live in slow motion?" Mel cracked, poking his sweaty head through the window.

"It's so busy tonight," Heather said.

"If it's so busy, why'd you let the old lady sit by herself in a booth for six?"

"Sorry."

She was so tired of apologizing to Mel. It seemed as if she spent half her time in the restaurant apologizing.

I've got to quit this job. I've got to get out of here, Heather thought, before I totally lose my mind.

After work, Snowman was waiting for her beside her car.

"Hi!" she called excitedly and started running across the empty lot.

As she came closer, she saw that he had a wide grin on his face. Maybe he has good news, she thought.

He came hurrying toward her. They met in the middle of the vast lot.

"You look like a Smile button tonight," she said.

"Well, I feel pretty good," he said, still grinning.

"Tell me," Heather said eagerly. "Tell me what's happening!"

They had been walking to her car as they talked. He leaned back against the side of the trunk. It was warm enough that he wore his overcoat unbuttoned. He had on a red flannel shirt underneath.

"Come *on*. Don't keep me in suspense," Heather pleaded, giving him a playful shove, pushing him back against the car. "What's going on? Where've you been all week? Why are you grinning like that?"

His grin slowly faded. He leaned way forward and pretended to fall off the car to the ground.

"You're goofy tonight," she said, pulling him up.

"Come on, Snowman. Are you going to talk or are you just going to clown around?"

He leaned back against the car, his hands in his coat pockets. "You did me a favor the other night," he told her, "so I returned the favor."

"Huh? You *what*?"

"I returned the favor." Suddenly he was completely serious.

"What do you mean?" Heather was puzzled. Why was he being so mysterious?

"You don't have to worry about your uncle anymore."

He wasn't making any sense to her. No sense at all.

"Snowman — what are you talking about?"

"I told you. I told you I could handle your uncle, right?"

"Yes, you said that, but — what do you mean?"

His smile returned. His eyes seemed to light up.

"I killed him, Heather. I killed him. For you."

Chapter 17

"Snowman — come on. That's not funny."

Heather stared into his dark eyes, studied his face, looking for a hint that he was teasing.

But his face revealed nothing. His eyes were like glass, dark and secretive. He looked back at her coolly, watching her reaction, showing no emotion at all.

Cold as ice.

"You're joking — right?"

Heather's legs suddenly felt weak. She leaned against the car hood. Snowman shifted his weight, then moved in front of her.

A black car pulled into the lot, cruising slowly past the darkened stores. Snowman watched its progress, his features tensing. He didn't relax until the car had passed them and was pulling out of the lot.

"No. I'm not joking," he said quietly. "Why would I joke about something like that?"

"Listen, Snowman. Enough."

"I handled him for you, Heather."

"But I didn't — I mean — "

"It was so easy," Snowman said, smiling for the first time. A look of disappointment shaded his face when she didn't smile back.

"This is the grossest joke," she said. It wasn't true. It couldn't be true.

"Stop saying that it's a joke," he snapped, bending his head and rubbing the back of his neck. "I handled him. Like I said."

"But come on — "

"You always think it's going to be hard. But it never is," he said, studying her face.

It never is? she thought.

Has he done this before?

"I knocked on the front door. Then I just waited on the porch. He saw me, stepped out, and — *gotcha!*" Snowman tugged hard at his scarf, as if demonstrating. "It was that easy."

Heather felt sick. She realized she was starting to tremble all over. The parking lot began to tilt and spin.

"I used this red scarf," Snowman said, talking calmly, nonchalantly, as if telling her about a sports play he had seen or a movie. "I just tightened it around his neck. It was a real soft scarf. Real wool. So it didn't leave any mark."

"Snowman, please — stop — "

"Everyone will think he had a heart attack. They won't look for anything else. No problem." He smiled at her reassuringly.

She looked down at the car hood. She was gripping the door handle so tightly her hand hurt.

"Why do you look so upset?" he asked, putting a hand on her shoulder.

She shivered.

"Your problems are over, Heather. You should be happy." He put his hand under her chin and raised her head, forcing her to look at him. "You should be happy. I . . . I thought you'd be happy."

She pulled away. He lowered his hand, his expression more bewildered than hurt.

He's crazy, she thought.

He really doesn't understand why I'm upset.

He just killed my uncle, murdered him in cold blood, and he expects me to be happy and thank him.

"Tell me this is all a stupid joke," she said, her voice trembling.

"Come on, Heather. I guess you're from Missouri."

"What do you mean?"

"It's the Show Me State. I guess you won't believe me till I show you."

She stood staring at him. Her mouth felt dry. It was hard to swallow.

I'm going to be sick, she thought.

Suddenly all of the smells in the air, all of the

smells around her became exaggerated. She could smell the french fry grease in her hair. She could smell the oil vapors from a puddle of motor oil on the parking lot near her feet.

What's happening to me? she thought.

"Come on. Unlock the car," Snowman said cheerfully. "Let's go to your house. Let's go see if your uncle has had that fatal heart attack or not."

Her hand was shaking so badly, she had trouble unlocking the car door. Sighing loudly, she slid behind the wheel, grateful to be sitting down.

Can I drive? she wondered. Her heart was pounding so hard, the blood was throbbing in her forehead.

Snowman tapped the window on the passenger side. "Come on — open up!"

I shouldn't let him in, she thought. I should drive off without him.

But she pulled up the door lock. He opened the door and climbed in quickly.

The car started on the third try.

"Okay, let's bomb out of here!" he said enthusiastically.

Why is he putting me on like this? Heather wondered.

Why does he think it's funny to continue this dreadful joke?

It *is* a joke. It has to be.

He didn't *really* kill Uncle James — *did* he?

Chapter 18

Heather's front yard seemed to be flickering on and off. First she could see the snow illuminated in pink. Then everything went black. Then pink. Then black.

It took her a long while to realize that the flashing light was on top of the square white ambulance. And the square white ambulance was parked at the head of the driveway.

"Oh, no."

She took a deep breath, pulled the car to the curb, and jumped out without even turning off the ignition.

The porch light was on, casting its cone of yellow light onto the uniformed men who seemed to be huddled on the front porch, frozen there like shadowy statues, not moving at all.

As Heather ran up the drive, she began to hear their muted voices. She saw that they were bent over something. A body. Her uncle's body.

"No. No."

And there was her aunt in the doorway. Her aunt was waving to her, her hand high in the air.

What was that in her aunt's hand?

It was a handkerchief.

The body was covered with a sheet.

The yellow porch light made everyone seem out-of-focus, strange. Aunt Belle continued to wave, even though Heather had acknowledged it.

Heather ran as fast as she could, her sneakers slipping on the slushy snow as she crossed the yard and ran onto the porch, joining the shadowy figures, joining the unreal scene in the yellow light.

And then Aunt Belle was reaching up and wrapping Heather in her arms. And crying.

She feels so bony, Heather thought.

What a strange thing to be thinking about.

But what *are* you supposed to be thinking about when your uncle is lying dead on the porch and you know that your boyfriend killed him?

"He went suddenly," Aunt Belle said, burying her face in Heather's shoulder, holding onto Heather so tightly she couldn't breathe. "At least it was quick. That's what I keep telling myself."

"Aunt Belle — when did it happen?" Heather asked. Her aunt smelled like lilacs from the toilet water she used. Heather had never noticed it before.

"That's the way he always wanted to go," Aunt Belle said, not hearing Heather's question. "He always said, 'When I go, I want to go quickly.' So I'm glad he got his wish. I'm just so sorry it happened so . . . early."

She broke down into loud sobs and would have fallen if Snowman hadn't stepped from behind Heather and caught her.

"I'm so sorry," he said softly, holding onto Heather's aunt. "I'm so sorry."

Heather realized she had forgotten all about Snowman.

Aunt Belle was crying into his shoulder now, and he was talking to her in a low, soothing voice.

Suddenly his eye caught Heather's. His expression chilled her to the bone.

It wasn't an expression of remorse. It wasn't an expression that said, "Sorry I've caused your aunt this pain."

It was an expression of triumph. Of amusement.

I told you so. That's what Snowman's face was saying.

I told you so, but you wouldn't believe me.

He's a murderer, she thought. And for the first time she thought she understood what people meant when they said a *cold-blooded* murderer.

"We were finishing dinner," Aunt Belle said, still sobbing. "He thought he heard a knock on the door. I didn't even hear it. He got up and went to see. And then . . . he didn't come back."

"Maybe you should go in and sit down," Snowman said gently, glancing at Heather.

"That's where I found him." Aunt Belle didn't seem to be able to hear anything anyone said to her.

"That's where I found him. He went just like that. So quick. It was so quick."

"Looks like cardiac arrest," one of the white-uniformed men said. "Mark this D.O.A., Mitch." He stood up and, straightening his coat, walked up to Aunt Belle, who was still clinging to Snowman.

"He went real quick, didn't he?" Aunt Belle asked.

She sounds like a little girl, Heather thought. She could smell something burning, some kind of meat. It was probably coming from next door.

"We have to go now," the paramedic said quietly.

"But — what about James?" Aunt Belle asked, not looking down at the covered corpse of her husband.

"We can't move it, er, him," the man said. "Do you have a funeral parlor? They will come out and pick him up for you."

"Well, no . . ." Heather's aunt started to fall apart again. "I don't know. We . . . I mean I . . ."

"Come inside," Snowman said, holding her around the shoulders. "Come inside and sit down. Heather and I will help you make the arrangements."

"You're a nice boy," Aunt Belle said, leaning against him, allowing him to guide her into the living room.

The words sickened Heather.

A nice boy?

He was a murderer.

A *cold-blooded* murderer.

He had killed Uncle James. And here he was, saying soothing things to Aunt Belle, leading her into the house with his murderous hands wrapped around her.

"Sorry," the paramedic said to Heather. They had gathered all of their equipment. Heads down, the two of them stepped out of the eerie yellow light into the flashing pink and black night and walked quickly back to the ambulance.

Forcing down a wave of nausea, Heather stared at the covered corpse at her feet. Is that really Uncle James? she thought.

Is it possible that I'm never going to see him again? Never going to hear that high-pitched voice taunting me again?

She was tempted to pull back the sheet, to look at him one more time.

I've never seen a dead body, she thought. Uncle James is lying here dead on the porch.

I hated him so much. I wished him dead a million times. I dreamed about it. I fantasized about it.

Is that why I'm not glad?

Because I feel so guilty?

Is that why I feel so sick?

No. That isn't why.

Uncle James is lying here dead at my feet — and his murderer is sitting in the living room with my aunt.

His murderer. My boyfriend.

My boyfriend. The murderer.

"Ohh." She moaned aloud.

Moving unsteadily to the door, Heather stumbled on the sheet, and the sheet unfurled at the top.

Uncle James stared up at her, wide-eyed, his face yellow-orange in the porch light.

His thin-lipped mouth was wide open, frozen in a look of horror and surprise. He stared up accusingly at Heather, his eyes as blank and cold as . . . Snowman's.

"No!"

Heather tore open the door and lurched inside, not stopping to pull the sheet back over her uncle's face.

In the brightly lit living room, Aunt Belle was on the couch, crying softly into a handkerchief. Snowman sat on the other end of the couch, his hands folded in his lap.

Heather stepped reluctantly into the room, trying to clear her head, trying to think of what to do.

I have to get Snowman out of here.

No. I have to call the police.

He can't get away with this. Everyone has to know that he killed my uncle.

No. I have to get him away from here first. Then I'll be able to think of how to handle this.

Handle this?

"I handled your uncle." She could hear Snowman out on the parking lot. "I handled your uncle." He said it with such ease, such pride.

"I — I'll get the phone book," Heather said. "I'll find a funeral parlor."

If I concentrate on practical matters, on getting things done, I won't think about Snowman, Heather decided. And I'll be able to get through this.

Maybe.

She found a funeral parlor, phoned it, and arranged for her uncle's body to be picked up. Then she made a pot of tea and served some to Aunt Belle and to Snowman and herself.

The tea warmed her a little. Her trembling stopped.

But she felt a stab of fear every time she looked at Snowman and saw him staring back at her.

"It's getting so late," she said, after the men had come and carried Uncle James's corpse into their van. "Would you like to go to bed, Aunt Belle?"

Her aunt shook her head. "I think I'll just sit here for a while. Why don't you go on up, Heather? I'll be fine."

Aunt Belle turned to Snowman, who was still seated beside her on the couch, and squeezed his hand. "You've been so nice, Bill. Thank you."

"No need to thank me," Bill said softly. He stood up. "I'll come by tomorrow and see if you need anything."

He started to the door, picking up his overcoat, which he had draped over an armchair. Heather followed him to the front hallway.

"I can't believe you stayed around," she whispered angrily.

His eyes widened in surprise. "What?"

"You can't get away with this," Heather said,

forcing herself to keep her voice low enough that Aunt Belle wouldn't hear. "You're crazy. You're really crazy. You need help!"

Now he looked hurt. "I don't understand."

"Ssshh. Lower your voice. I don't want her to hear."

"Heather — I don't *understand*."

"That's the problem, Snowman. Or Bill. Or whoever you really are. You murdered someone. You murdered my uncle. And you think you didn't do anything wrong."

"But, Heather — come on. I did it for you."

"Don't say that. I mean it."

"But you hated him! You told me you hated him. You told me you wished he was dead. You said it all the time."

"But that didn't mean you should go do it," Heather cried, feeling herself start to lose control. "Sure, I hated him. But you can't just *kill* people."

"You'll feel better tomorrow," Snowman said, leaning against the wooden banister.

"No, I won't," Heather said, shutting her eyes, seeing her uncle's yellow, staring face again. "No, I won't feel better. You just don't understand, do you, Snowman? You killed my uncle. You waited out there and you murdered him."

"Yeah?"

"So I have to call the police."

"What?"

"I have to call the police. I don't have a choice."

He laughed.

It was a cold laugh, a laugh she'd never heard from him before.

"Why on earth are you laughing?"

"You can't call the police," he said, still laughing. "There's no way you can call the police."

Chapter 19

"What do you *mean* I can't call the police?" Heather demanded, hating the smug smile on Snowman's face. "All I have to do is walk over to the phone and dial 911."

Snowman started to answer her, but Aunt Belle interrupted, surprising them by appearing behind them in the hallway. "I think I *will* go up to my room," she said, her eyes red and watery. "I probably won't be able to sleep, but I'd like to lie down."

Heather and Snowman said good night to her, and both watched in silence as she made her way up the stairs. When she was in her room, Heather walked back into the living room, her arms crossed over her chest. She pressed her arms against herself tightly, as if trying to hold herself together.

She knew she had to hold herself back or she would go roaring out of control. She felt like screaming, screaming her lungs out, or tearing something apart.

Snowman walked coolly into the room, his expression still smug, almost pleased with himself.

"So what makes you think I won't go to the police?" She repeated her question, forcing her voice to remain steady.

"You can't," Snowman said. "Because of this." He reached into the pocket of his flannel shirt and held up a rectangular sheet of green paper.

"What's that?"

"Don't you recognize it, Heather? It's the check. The check you wrote me for two thousand dollars."

"What about it?" Heather felt confused. What did the check have to do with her not being able to report him to the police?

He grinned at her, a very pleased, self-satisfied grin. "If you turn me in to the police, I show them this check."

"And?"

"And I tell them that this is what you paid me to murder your uncle."

"No!"

Heather hadn't meant to scream so loudly. She didn't want to disturb Aunt Belle. But she couldn't help herself.

He'd planned it. He'd planned it all. He tricked me into writing that check so that he could implicate me in the murder he *planned* to commit. How could he be so *evil*? she thought.

"Why would the police believe a story like that?"

she asked, suddenly more angry than upset.

"Heather, get real. Why *wouldn't* they believe it? Here's a check made out to me for two thousand dollars. It *had* to be a payoff. Why else would you give me all that money?"

"But you *know* why I gave it to you," Heather cried. "For your brother."

Snowman's face filled with amusement. "Well," he said, "you'd better not tell the police *that* story. I don't have a brother."

"You — you don't?"

"No. And I don't have a mother who's a nurse. And I don't go to your stupid high school."

"So nothing was true," Heather said, sitting down on the arm of the nearest chair, feeling a little dazed.

"One thing *is* true," he said. He held up the check. "This is true. This check made out to me is true. It's my insurance policy. It's my insurance that you'll never say a word to anyone about me."

He tucked the check back into his shirt pocket. "I'm keeping it forever," he said. "Right here. Right by my heart."

"That check is no kind of proof," Heather said, realizing she sounded desperate. "The police will believe me if I tell them the truth."

"No, they won't," Snowman said, slipping into his overcoat. "Everyone knows you hated your uncle. Even your best friends would testify to that."

"Now, wait — "

"Everyone has seen you fight with him. Everyone has heard you say you wished he were dead. You must have said it a million times, Heather. The police will believe that you paid me to kill him. There's no way they wouldn't believe me."

He buttoned the coat calmly, slowly, watching her horrified reaction to what he was saying, enjoying it. "So forget about the police, Heather. Wipe that idea from your head. That thought is dead, right? As dead as dear old Uncle James."

"Just go away," Heather said bitterly. She turned her back on him. "Go away before I scream."

"We're in this together," he said, walking to the front door. "Don't forget that, Heather. We're in it together."

Chapter 20

The funeral on Saturday was held in a small chapel on North Side, near the cemetery. The room was nearly filled with people, most of them around Heather's uncle's age. She was genuinely surprised to see that he had so many friends, so many people who cared enough about him to come to his funeral.

Aunt Belle, looking pale in her black dress and even more frail than ever, held herself together through the service, dabbing at her eyes with a tissue held in a shaky hand, seldom looking up.

Heather sat beside her on the bench, occasionally reaching over to squeeze her aunt's hand reassuringly or slip her another tissue.

"I'm so sorry," a voice said. Heather looked up to see Kim standing above her. Kim's eyes searched Heather's face, as if trying to determine how upset Heather was.

"Hi. Thanks for coming," Heather said quietly.

Everyone seemed to be whispering this morning.

They're afraid they might wake up Uncle James, and no one wants him back!

She scolded herself for having such an evil thought.

But it was hard to control your mind at a funeral, she was discovering. It kept jumping around, thinking the most unpredictable things.

"Maybe we can talk later," Kim said, and walked up the aisle to take a seat near the back.

Waiting for the service to begin, finding it hard to sit still, Heather turned back to see who else was in the chapel. She was surprised to see Ben sitting on the aisle a few rows behind her. She nodded to him and mouthed the word *hi*. He gave her a wave. He looked very uncomfortable.

He even wore a tie, Heather thought. She realized she wanted to talk to Ben. She *needed* to talk to Ben.

". . . offer my condolences."

A voice broke into Heather's thoughts, made her turn back to the front.

Snowman was standing in front of her, wearing a dark shirt buttoned all the way up to the collar and dark brown corduroy trousers. He was leaning down, talking quietly to Aunt Belle.

Heather felt all of her muscles tighten in anger.

How can he have the nerve to show up here?

How can the murderer come to the funeral? What is he trying to prove?

Heather had trouble swallowing. Her throat suddenly felt dry. Her hands were ice-cold. She wanted to jump up and strangle Snowman, choke away that phony look of concern from his face.

To her horror, Aunt Belle patted the empty spot on the bench beside her, inviting Snowman to sit down.

Look at him, Heather thought, filled with revulsion watching the solemn, sympathetic look on Snowman's face as he sat down on the other side of her aunt.

Like he's one of the family.

How sickening.

She had the sudden impulse to lean over and whisper to Aunt Belle that Snowman had murdered her husband. She had the impulse to jump up and stand in front of everyone and announce that Snowman was a murderer, a cold-blooded murderer.

He leaned forward, his hands gripping the bench seat, and smiled at her.

She angrily turned her head.

The minister came out, and the room grew quiet.

Heather stared at the open coffin to the left of the minister. The coffin was draped with white carnations. Uncle James's head poked up, rouged-pink and shiny, through the carnations.

I really did hate him, Heather thought.

I really did want him to die.

But I didn't want him killed.

The minister droned on. His voice echoed off the walls of the small chapel. Heather didn't hear a word he said.

Staring at the pink head of her uncle, she tried to think of what she should do now, what she should do about Snowman.

It was a raw, gray afternoon. Standing in the cemetery, watching the casket being lowered into the ground, Heather thought she was about to freeze to death.

I'm as cold as Uncle James, she thought, jamming her hands into the pockets of her blue wool coat, trying to stop shivering.

More carnations were tossed into the grave. The minister had more to say. His words seemed to catch in the frozen air. The sounds never reached Heather's ears.

Then everything became a slow-motion blur. People coming up to offer condolences, handshakes, and hugs, quiet testimonies from friends and strangers about how untimely Uncle James's death was.

Heather stood beside her aunt, her arm round the little woman's narrow waist, trying to offer support, trying to help get her through this long, cold, dreary afternoon. When Snowman came up to her, Heather turned away again. She saw Ben standing on the walk on the other side of the grave, and hurried over to him.

"Hi," she said with a shiver.

"Hi," he repeated, still looking as uncomfortable as he had inside.

"You wore a tie," she said, reaching up and giving the knot a tug.

"My mom made me," he said. "How are you doing?"

"Okay." Heather rocked up and down on her shoes. "I hated my uncle, but this is sad."

"Sad for your aunt," Ben said, brushing his dark hair back off his forehead.

"Yeah." Heather turned back and saw that Snowman had taken her place beside Aunt Belle. Now he had his arm around her waist and was shaking hands with people who came up to them.

"I'd like to kill him," Heather said.

"What did you say?" Ben stared at her, his face filled with concern.

"Oh. Sorry. I didn't mean to talk aloud." Heather could feel her face getting hot. "Could we . . . uh . . . talk later?"

"Yeah. Good." Ben gave her a shy smile.

"I'll call you tomorrow. Okay?"

"Sounds good."

I want to tell you about how Snowman murdered my uncle and how he says he'll implicate me in the murder if I go to the police.

That's what Heather *wanted* to say.

But she knew she couldn't.

Instead, she gave Ben a quick, awkward kiss on the cheek and hurried back to pull her aunt out of Snowman's clutches.

* * *

Heather saw the black Taurus pull up the driveway.

She had been staring out the front window, pressing her forehead against the glass. It was a little after seven in the evening. The few people who had come to the house after the funeral for cake and coffee had left. Aunt Belle had gone up to her room to lie down.

Heather felt both weary and keyed-up at the same time, completely out-of-sorts. Her mind kept flitting from thought to thought, strange unconnected memories, complicated fantasies, like a bee hopping from flower to flower, never resting in any one place for more than a second.

The cold, gray images of the funeral kept playing again and again in her mind. And through the gray thoughts, the bright pink head of her uncle appeared, like a flowering weed sprouting up through a concrete sidewalk. And then everything faded to white, and she realized the white was the color of Snowman's hair.

And then, standing at the window, trapped by her thoughts, unable to push the sad, frightening pictures from her mind, she saw the yellow headlights move across the lawn.

She saw the car pull up the drive.

And she realized it was a black Taurus.

The same black Taurus that had followed her and frightened her that night?

She opened the front door to two men in almost

identical gray overcoats. They both were hatless despite the frigid night. Both had wavy, brown hair cut very short. Both were wearing almost identical, short, trimmed brown mustaches, and identical serious looks.

"Can I help you?" she called through the glass storm door.

Are they twins? she wondered.

What can they be selling?

The taller one pulled an ID card the size of a credit card out of his coat pocket and held it up at the door. "FBI, Miss," he said. His mouth didn't seem to move under his mustache. Both men stared straight ahead at Heather without blinking. "Can we come in?"

"Uh . . . why?"

"We just have a couple of questions to ask about someone you may know."

"It's been a long day," Heather said. A bit of an understatement. "Do you think you could come back?"

"It will only take a minute or two. Promise," the taller one said. His partner nodded. Neither of them had blinked yet.

Heather reluctantly unlocked the storm door, and they stepped into the front hall, carefully wiping their black wing-tipped shoes on the mat.

"I'm Special Agent Forbes, and this is Special Agent Mackey." He held up his ID card again but lowered it before Heather could really read it.

Are they putting me on? Heather wondered.

They certainly *looked* like FBI men. They were both such straight arrows.

But they were a little too perfect, Heather thought.

"Do you know a boy named William Jeffers?" the one named Forbes asked.

I don't believe it! Heather thought. Snowman actually told us his real name!

"Were you the ones who followed me after work the other night?" Heather asked. The question just tumbled out.

"Yes," Forbes answered quickly, reaching up to scratch one side of his mustache. "Sorry if we alarmed you."

"Why did you follow me?" Heather asked.

"We had reason to believe that you know William Jeffers. We followed you to find out where you lived. We didn't want to bother you at your job."

"Thank you," Heather said sarcastically. "You scared me to death." She was thinking hard, trying to decide how much to tell these two men.

If they are FBI, she thought, I don't want to tell them anything. I don't want to help them. Because then Snowman will show them the check.

My life will be ruined.

Those words ran through her mind.

My life will be ruined. Because of that creep.

"Who did you want to ask me about?" She decided to pretend she didn't know him.

"William Jeffers."

She pretended to think about it, then shook her head. "No. Sorry. I don't know anyone by that name."

"He's tall. About a head taller than you. He has white hair," Forbes said, staring into her eyes, studying her face.

Mackey coughed and cleared his throat several times.

"White hair . . . hmm. . . ." Maybe they've seen me with him, Heather thought. I'd better not play too dumb. They'll know I'm lying.

"Hey — a boy with white hair came into the restaurant," she said, pretending to suddenly remember. "It was weird. His hair, I mean."

"When was that?" Forbes asked.

"A couple of weeks ago, I guess."

"And have you seen him since?"

"Uh . . . yeah. He waited for me after work one night. He tried to pick me up."

"Did you go out with him?"

"No. I told him no, and he went away. I've never seen him again."

"Are you sure?" Mackey said, speaking for the first time.

"Yes, I'm sure. He was kind of creepy, I think. What did you say his name was?"

"Jeffers. William Jeffers."

"He didn't tell me his name," Heather said. She wondered if they were buying her story. Neither of them had changed expression. They both stared at her, their faces like masks, revealing nothing.

"Is there anything else you can tell us about William Jeffers?" Forbes asked.

Heather pretended to think hard. I'd better tell them something, she thought. "Yes. He was wearing an old-fashioned-type overcoat. Very big. Very fifties. That's about all I remember about him."

Except for the fact that he murdered my uncle and will tell you that I paid him to do it if you catch him, she thought, suddenly feeling very tired.

"And you only saw him that one night at the restaurant?"

"Yeah. Just that night," Heather lied.

She heard a creaking noise upstairs. She hoped Aunt Belle wasn't coming down. Having two FBI agents in the house would really upset her. And how could Heather ever explain?

"Sorry to intrude today," Forbes said, bowing his head somberly. "I know there's been a death in the family."

"We won't keep you any longer," Mackey added, pushing open the storm door.

A blast of cold air invaded the entranceway.

"If you see him again, please call this number," Forbes said, handing her a small card.

"Okay," Heather said, starting to feel relieved that they were leaving. She didn't know how much longer she could go on lying to them. "Oh. How come you're looking for him?" she asked.

"Murder," Forbes said quietly. "He killed his father."

Chapter 21

"Hi, Kim. Yeah, I have the assignment. Hold on. I'll get it."

Heather put down her new phone and walked across her bedroom to the desk to find the English assignment for Kim. I've got to put away my new clothes, she thought, seeing the pile of things on top of her dresser.

She read Kim the assignment, then hung up.

Life has certainly improved in the three weeks since the funeral, she thought. For one thing, it was so peaceful, so pleasant around the house without Uncle James.

For another, Heather didn't have to live as if she were a poor orphan any longer. Aunt Belle had turned over control of her trust fund to her. "You have to promise you'll be careful with the money," Aunt Belle had said. "It's all you have in the world, Heather."

Heather had promised. And she was determined to keep her promise. But she did need new clothes to finish off the winter, and a phone for her room, which she got. Those were absolute necessities.

There were two other reasons why Heather was beginning to feel pretty good. One was that she planned to quit her job at the restaurant tonight.

The other was that she hadn't seen Snowman since the day of her uncle's funeral.

Maybe he's left town, she thought hopefully.

Maybe he knows the FBI is after him. Maybe he's gone for good, run off to a place where he hopes they won't find him.

Yes. Gone for good.

I'll never see him again.

As she thought these reassuring thoughts, the new phone rang.

It's him, she thought, her hand hesitating on the receiver. It's Snowman.

She had a heavy feeling in the pit of her stomach as she lifted the receiver to her ear. "Hello?"

"Hi, Heather. It's me."

"Ben?" She breathed a loud sigh of relief.

"How's it going?" he asked.

"Great! I mean, okay. Not bad."

"Should I pick A, B, C, or all of the above?" he cracked.

They both laughed.

Ben can always make me laugh, she thought.

"What are you doing?" he asked.

"Going to the restaurant to quit my job."

"That sounds like fun." He was silent for a few seconds. "Want to go to the movies or something tomorrow night?"

She didn't have to think about it. "Sure," she said.

"Yeah? I mean, good. I'll come by around seven-thirty. Have fun quitting your job."

"Thanks." She hung up feeling really happy.

An hour later, she told Mel this would be her last night as a waitress. He pretended not to care. Marjorie said, "I'll miss you, Heather. Come in for a Coke sometime, okay?"

Heather didn't really plan to go into the restaurant ever again.

After work, she pulled off the dorky uniform for the last time and left it in a corner of the ladies' room. She put on her street clothes, walked across the emptying parking lot to her car, and saw Snowman leaning against the hood.

"Surprise," he said, without smiling.

Chapter 22

"What do *you* want?" Heather said. She felt as if she were sinking, sinking below the surface of the ocean. She suddenly felt so heavy, as if a giant rock had been placed on top of her.

Or a gravestone.

Seeing him standing against her car again, all of the horror came back. The coldness. The guilt. The death . . .

"What kind of greeting is that?" he asked, his face blank, expressionless, his eyes burning into hers.

"Please. What do you want? I don't want to see you." She jammed her hands into the pockets of her new down ski jacket.

The night sky, she realized, was pink, as pink as her dead uncle's forehead. It felt as if it were about to snow.

"Well, you have to see me," he said coldly. "I'm here."

"Men are looking for you," she said, hoping to frighten him just a little.

He reached out and grabbed her collar. "New coat?"

Heather pulled back, out of his grasp. "Stop."

"Nice. Looks expensive."

"Snowman — it's cold out here. What do you want?" she asked impatiently.

"What did you tell the men who are after me?" It sounded more like an accusation than a question.

"Nothing."

"What did you tell them?" His eyes narrowed, cold and mean.

Heather shivered. "Nothing. I told them I didn't know you."

Snowman laughed.

"Really. That's what I said."

"Oh, they'll really believe that," he said, pulling his lips back in a sneer. "Why do you think they came to see you? Because they probably saw us together."

"I told them you came into the restaurant once, that you waited for me and tried to pick me up. That's all I said. You've got to believe me. I'm telling you the truth."

He killed his father, she thought.

Killed his father. And my uncle.

"I thought you and me had something going," he said, his face softening.

"No!"

He looked hurt. "Okay, okay. I can take a hint."

A wailing siren made them both turn to the street beyond the parking lot. A black-and-white police car went roaring through a red light and down the service road.

"What do you want?" Heather asked. "It's cold out here."

"Well, I guess I need some money."

"Money? From me? I already wrote you a check."

"But I can't cash it." He patted his coat over his shirt pocket. "I keep it right here, remember? As a memento." He chuckled.

"How much do you want?" Heather asked wearily. "How much do you want to go away and never come back again?"

"Well, I guess two thousand dollars." He didn't have to think about it. He obviously already had the amount in mind. "You know. The amount of the first check."

"And if I write you a check for two thousand dollars, I'll never see you or hear from you again?"

He raised his right hand as if swearing an oath. "Yeah. Sure. You write me a check, and if the check clears, and I get the two thousand, you'll never see me again."

"Promise?"

"Hey — don't call me a liar, Heather!" he snapped, suddenly, instantly angry.

She took a step back. She'd never seen him erupt like that before.

"Okay," she said, deciding quickly. "I'll do it."

"That's better." His features were still tight with anger. He brushed his white hair back out of his eyes. "That's better. You got your checkbook?"

She nodded and started to dig through her bag.

"Hurry up." He looked nervously toward the street. Another police car sped past.

Losing your cool, huh, Snowman? Heather thought. Not cold as ice anymore.

She felt such hatred for him now. The sight of him made her feel sick. She couldn't believe that she had really cared about him just a few weeks before.

Pulling the checkbook from her bag, she leaned onto the hood of the car. Her hand was trembling as she started to write.

"Make it out to cash," he said.

One check, just two thousand dollars, and I'll never see him again, she thought.

What a laugh.

I'll see him every time I close my eyes. Every time I think of my uncle. I'll see Snowman for the rest of my life. I'll see him and feel the guilt, see him and have this same sick feeling. . . .

Heather signed the check and tore it from the checkbook.

Snowman grabbed it from her hand before she could give it to him. "No tricks," he said warily. "If this bounces, I'll be back."

"No tricks," she said, suddenly weary. "Just take the money and go away."

He looked hurt. "Well, okay. If that's the way you feel about it."

"Stop smirking at me like that!" Heather screamed, losing control. "You murdered my uncle! You killed a man and it doesn't mean anything to you! It was like swatting a fly! You're sick! You need help!"

He angrily grabbed her arm. His eyes flared for a brief second, then immediately cooled. "I don't need help," he said through clenched teeth. "I help myself."

"Let go of me, Snowman."

"You think your uncle was such a bad dude? You should've grown up in my house. You should've grown up with my dad. I can tell you about a bad dude, Heather. I can tell you about having it rough at home. I've got the scars to prove it. Deep scars. Real scars. Not mental scars. Real scars."

"Snowman, please — "

"Your uncle ever beat you?"

"No. He — "

"Your uncle ever take a bicycle chain from the garage and beat you with it till you were bleeding?"

"Snowman — "

"Your uncle ever tie you to a tree and leave you outside all night because you talked back to him?"

"Oh, how awful — "

"I don't need help, Heather. *You* needed help, and I helped you." He waved the check in front of her face. "And now you're helping me back."

He seemed to calm down. His face went blank again. The angry glow faded from his eyes. He folded the check and shoved it into the back pocket of his jeans.

"Good-bye, Snowman," Heather said, searching for the car key in her bag, eager to escape, to never see him again.

"Good-bye forever," he said bitterly.

Then he suddenly grabbed her shoulders, startling her, and pushed his lips against hers. "A good-bye kiss," he said, when he let her go. Then he turned and jogged away into the darkness.

Heather shuddered. His lips were so cold. Cold as ice.

She stood watching him run across the empty parking lot until he disappeared around a corner of the mall. He never looked back.

"Yeah, right, Kim. I know. I'm real happy about it, too."

It was a week later. Tuesday evening. Heather, on the phone up in her room, played carelessly with her blonde ponytail as she told Kim how happy she was that she and Ben were going together again.

"I know. He's really funny. But I was so mad. He knows how easy it is to crack me up. So why'd he have to do it while I was giving my oral book report? It was so embarrassing. I — Oh, hold on a minute, Kim."

Aunt Belle was calling from downstairs.

"Be down in a minute!" Heather shouted, looking at her desk clock. It was nearly six. "Guess it's time for dinner," she told Kim. "I'll call you later, okay?"

She hung up and, giving her hair a quick brush and straightening her sweatshirt, went downstairs to see what her aunt had prepared for dinner. "Hey, Aunt Belle — why did you use the fancy placemats tonight?"

"It's a surprise," Aunt Belle said, a mischievous look on her face.

"Hey — you set three places."

"We're having a guest," Aunt Belle said, putting the forks down beside the plates. "A surprise guest."

The doorbell rang before Heather had a chance to guess who it might be.

She pulled open the door and gasped.

Snowman entered, a broad smile on his face, looking past Heather to Aunt Belle.

"Surprise!" Aunt Belle exclaimed. "Bill called earlier and I invited him to dinner. Wipe your feet and come in, Bill," she said warmly. "Dinner is ready. We haven't seen enough of you lately."

"Thanks," Snowman said, turning his gaze on Heather, the pleased smile still plastered on his face.

"You're a liar," Heather whispered angrily through gritted teeth. "You're a filthy liar."

He grinned at her. "Does that surprise you?"

Chapter 23

"I'm just going upstairs and watch some TV," Aunt Belle said, smiling warmly at Snowman. "It was nice to see you, Bill. Thanks for coming."

"It was a great dinner," Snowman said.

"And thanks for repairing that ceiling fixture," Heather's aunt said, halfway up the stairs. "It's so hard for me these days. James used to do all the repairs, of course. Now . . ." Her voice trailed off sadly.

"I'll come real soon and fix the basement railing," Snowman called up to her from the living room couch.

"Oh, you don't have to do that. I'll call a carpenter and — "

"No trouble. Really," Snowman said, turning his glance on Heather, who was sitting stiffly in the armchair across the room. "I enjoy doing it. I'll call you this week about that other thing we talked about."

Aunt Belle disappeared into her room.

"What other thing?" Heather whispered angrily.

"Come over here. I can't hear you," Snowman said, patting the couch cushion next to him.

"Get real. I just want you out of here," Heather said, so furious she could barely contain herself.

"Come *over* here," he insisted. "I won't bite. Really."

Won't bite? You're a *murderer*, Heather thought.

Don't you even *know* you're a murderer? Are you so crazy that you think you can come in here and act like a normal person?

Won't bite? You're a murderer, murderer, murderer.

She got up and walked slowly across the room, standing over him, her arms crossed, glaring down at him. "What are you doing here? Why did you come back? You promised."

"I know. I know," he whispered. "Sit down, please. You're making me nervous."

He didn't look the least bit nervous, Heather saw. In fact, he looked quite calm and pleased with himself.

She sat down tensely on the arm of the couch, as far away from him as she could get. "Answer my questions. What are you doing here? What do you want?"

"Maybe I just want a little friendliness," he said softly.

"Cut the bull, Snowman."

"Yeah. Well. Okay. Twenty guesses why I'm here."

"You need more money."

"You got it, ace. First guess."

"You're crazy. You're really crazy," Heather said, shaking her head. She suddenly realized she was terrified of him. Behind her anger, behind her fury, lay a deep, cold well of fear.

He could kill me, too, she thought.

As easy as look at me.

"I'm not crazy," he said calmly, his expression going blank.

"Why would I give you more money?" Heather demanded. "Why?"

"You want to get rid of me. Right?"

"Yes."

"You want me to go away and never come back. Right?"

"Right. I think I made that clear."

"Well . . ."

She waited for him to finish his sentence, staring angrily into his dark eyes.

"Well, one more check, and I'll disappear."

"I don't believe you," Heather said, trying not to let him see how frightened she was.

"I'm telling the truth. One more check. Then I'll be out of your life. You can forget you ever saw me.

You can forget that I was the one who helped you out, who helped you handle your . . . problem."

"How much do you want this time?" Heather asked reluctantly.

Again, he didn't hesitate. "Five thousand." His expression remained blank.

"Five thousand dollars? You want a check for five thousand dollars?"

"No. Cash. I need it in cash this time."

Heather didn't say anything. She looked down at the floor. I just want to sink into the floor and die, she thought. I just want to disappear. I want to be a speck of dust and blow away.

"Well?" Snowman asked, sounding a little impatient for the first time.

"You really expect me to give you five thousand dollars?"

This isn't happening, she thought. I'm not really having this conversation.

"Yes," he said. "I do. You don't really have a choice, do you?"

Heather realized that he was right. She had no choice. If she refused, he could take her check to the police. He could tell them she paid to have her uncle killed.

Her life would be over.

She had no choice.

"What about those FBI men?" she asked, thinking hard. "Aren't they still after you? Aren't you afraid to be here?"

He shrugged. "I gave them the slip. They think I've split."

"You mean — ?"

"I mean they're not looking for me here anymore." He snickered. "They're not too bright, are they?"

Heather couldn't decide how she felt about this news. She didn't want Snowman to be caught because then he would implicate her. But she wanted him away, far away. She didn't want him sitting in her living room, looking at her with those cold, dark eyes, reminding her . . . frightening her. . . .

"If I give you the five thousand — "

"In cash," he interrupted.

"If I give it to you, will you really go away?"

"Yes," he said. He raised his hand as if taking an oath. "I'll put it in writing, if you want."

"I don't want anything in writing," Heather said, realizing she was about to give in.

Realizing she had no choice.

"I just want you gone."

"Okay, okay." He got up, looking annoyed. "You've made your point. You know, Heather, you really are an ungrateful little — "

"Shh. Quiet. Aunt Belle will hear." She jumped off the arm of the couch and took a few steps back, afraid that he was coming after her.

Glaring at her angrily, he raked a hand back through his thick, white hair.

He's trying to scare me, she thought.

It's just an act. He has no real emotion at all. Everything he does is just an act.

Which is the scariest thing of all.

"I don't have five thousand here," she said, whispering. "I'll have to go to the bank. The one by the old movie theater. You know. In town."

"When?" he asked.

"Tomorrow, I guess. I'll cut school in the morning."

"When does the bank open?"

"Nine, I guess."

"I'll meet you there at nine."

"Okay. I — "

"You won't do anything stupid, like call the police?" He patted his shirt pocket. "I keep it here, just like I said. Your check, Heather. My insurance policy."

"I won't call the police," she said, staring out the living room window. It had started to snow again. Large flakes falling rapidly. A real storm. "I'll give you the five thousand. And then — "

"I'll be gone," he said, his anger fading, a pleased smile spreading slowly across his face. "Snowman will just melt away."

"You promise?"

"Cross my heart." He crossed his fingers over his shirt pocket.

"Such a large amount," the tall, conservative-looking bank officer said, wrinkling his brow, studying Heather's signature as if it *had* to be a forgery.

"Yes. My aunt and I need it," Heather said.

What a lame excuse. But so what? she thought. It isn't any of his business.

"Maybe I should call your aunt to make sure about this," he said, lowering his head to look at her over the top of his glasses.

Oh, no, Heather thought.

He's going to ruin everything.

Snowman was waiting around the corner for his money. He had started to accompany her into the bank, then remembered all of the cameras installed there.

"I'm feeling a little camera-shy this morning," he had said. "You go in by yourself. I'll be waiting out here."

If this bank manager didn't hand over the money, what would Snowman do? And what would her aunt do if she got a call asking if it was okay for Heather to remove five thousand dollars from her trust fund?

"Uh . . . Aunt Belle isn't home," Heather lied. "But she asked me to bring the money to her right away."

"Then she should have sent a note along with you," he said crabbily, rubbing his long, narrow nose. "You are under legal age, after all."

"But the trust fund is entirely in my name," Heather argued, trying not to let her voice reveal how worried she was. "I'll tell you what. I'll take the money to my aunt, then bring you a note from her this afternoon."

You will forget all about it by this afternoon, Heather thought.

And Snowman will be gone forever by this afternoon.

The bank manager continued to rub his nose, staring at Heather as he thought it over. Finally he nodded his head. "Okay. How do you want it? Large bills?"

Heather secretly breathed a sigh of relief.

"Yeah. I guess. Hundreds will be okay."

The bank manager quickly countersigned the check and handed it back to her, still studying her face. "Take it to that teller over there."

A few minutes later, she was back out on Fair Street. The snowstorm had trickled down to an occasional flurry, having left a fresh six inches of snow on the ground during the night. The wind was cold and sharp, gusting around the corner of the bank as if in a hurry to get somewhere.

Snowman was sitting on a fire hydrant, the collar of his overcoat pulled up around his face. He stood up, pulling his red scarf tight when he saw Heather turn the corner.

"You get it?"

"Yes. Here it is. It's all in hundreds."

Heather handed him the legal-sized envelope.

He jammed the envelope into his overcoat pocket.

"Don't you even have a wallet or anything?" she asked.

"Guess I can afford to buy one now," he said.

" 'Bye." He turned and started walking quickly down the snow-covered sidewalk.

" 'Bye *forever*," Heather called pointedly.

She crossed the street and climbed into her car, feeling nervous and relieved all at the same time. Brushing the new snow off the windshield with the windshield wipers, she made a U-turn and headed toward school.

I'll be a few hours late. Big deal, she thought. I'll make some excuse. Like, I was getting five thousand dollars to pay off the boy who murdered my uncle.

She decided she couldn't face school. She drove past the low, brick building and just kept going.

She drove aimlessly in the snow all morning, stopped at a White Castle for lunch, then drove around most of the afternoon. At about three, she parked on a quiet road overlooking Swan Park, lay down on the front seat, and took a nap, sleeping uncomfortably, waking every few minutes unsure of where she was.

It was nearly six and dark as midnight when she pulled up the driveway to her house and ran inside. Aunt Belle was sitting alone in the darkened living room, staring out the front window.

"Sorry I'm late," Heather said quietly, turning on a lamp.

"I was worried about you," Aunt Belle said, turning around. She looked so pale and fragile, like a little girl, in the dim light from the lamp.

"I . . . uh . . . stopped at Kim's. I lost track of

the time," Heather said, rubbing her neck, which was stiff from lying in such an awkward position in the car.

"Well, go get washed up for dinner. I made meat loaf."

Heather walked over to the armchair in front of the window, bent down, and kissed her aunt on the forehead. Her aunt smelled of lilacs.

As she stood up, Heather saw something she hadn't noticed when she'd pulled up the drive. A light was on in the room on the top of the garage. "Aunt Belle — that light is on," she said, pointing.

"Yes." Aunt Belle smiled. "I rented the room just this afternoon."

"You rented the room in the garage? To whom?"

"To your friend. That nice boy Bill. Don't tell me you didn't know about it."

"Huh?" Heather wasn't sure she was hearing correctly. The dark room began to spin. Shadows danced on the walls.

"He surely must have told you he was going to rent the room," Aunt Belle insisted. "What do you two talk about anyway?"

"You mean you rented the room to — to — "

"To Bill Jeffers," Aunt Belle said, not noticing Heather's startled reaction. A pleased smile filled her face. "He gave me four hundred dollars in cash this afternoon. That's two full months' rent."

Chapter 24

"What can I do, Ben? He's going to keep taking my money. His promises don't mean a thing. I mean, there he is, living right above the garage."

"Try to calm down, Heather," Ben said, reaching his arm around her and pulling her closer to him on the living room couch. Once he had gotten over his shock at hearing Heather's story, he had quickly tried to comfort her.

It was ten-thirty in the evening, a few days after Snowman had made himself at home in the room above her aunt's garage. Aunt Belle had excused herself and gone up to her room. Heather decided she had no choice. She had to tell Ben. She had to confide in someone. She was desperate.

"Calm down? How can I calm down?" she whispered, not wanting her voice to carry upstairs. "He's in here all the time, fixing things for Aunt Belle, flirting with her, teasing her. It's so disgusting. If she only knew he killed her husband."

Ben took a deep breath. He always did that when he was thinking hard. "Heather, I really think — well — you have no choice, Heather. You have to go to the police," Ben said, grabbing her hand and rubbing it, trying to warm it. "You have to tell them the whole story."

"No, I —"

"They're looking for Snowman already, right? You said he murdered his father. So when they catch him, they're not going to believe his story. They're going to believe yours."

"No way," Heather wailed. "Don't you understand, Ben? I've given him *nine thousand dollars*. When the police find that out, they'll believe Snowman. They'll believe that I paid him to kill my uncle. Why wouldn't they believe it?" She turned away from him. "Oh, I was so stupid. How could I have been so stupid?"

"You wrote him three checks?" Ben asked, trying hard to get the whole story straight.

"Yes. But only one to his name. One was made out to cash. The rest I withdrew in cash from my trust fund."

"You only made one check out to his name?"

"Yeah. Why?"

"And he cashed it?"

"No," Heather said, sighing miserably. "That's the one he keeps as his insurance policy. That's the one he keeps with him all the time in his shirt pocket."

Ben got up and started pacing back and forth in front of her. He took a deep breath. "So if we got back that check . . ."

"Yeah?" Heather waited for him to finish his thought, her eyes trailing him back and forth across the gray living room rug.

"If we got back that check, there wouldn't be any proof that you had paid him."

"Well . . . not really," Heather replied, trying to figure out where Ben's mind was leading him. "There'd be the canceled check made out to cash, of course."

"But he could've stolen that, right?"

"I guess."

"That one check is the only thing tying you to him. So, we've got our answer," Ben said, stopping in front of the living room window, looking up to the room above the garage.

"You mean we go up there and steal the check from his shirt pocket?"

"Good idea," Ben said, still staring up to the garage. "Wish *I'd* thought of it."

Chapter 25

Watching from the living room window, they saw the light go out in Snowman's room. It was a little after eleven. They waited another half hour before pulling on their down jackets and creeping quietly out the front door.

The frigid night air felt good on Heather's face. They tried to walk silently down the front walk to the driveway, but a hard crust had formed over the deep snow, and their boots crunched loudly with each step.

Heather had turned the porch light off an hour earlier. The moon was covered by a thick curtain of clouds. The two-story garage loomed ahead of them, black against a blue-black sky.

"Go around to the side," Heather whispered to Ben. "If we open the front door, he'll hear us."

Ben turned back to her and nodded solemnly.

Even in the darkness, she could see the look of fear on his face.

She was trying to ignore her own fear, forcing herself forward, forcing herself to ignore the heavy feeling in her stomach, the pounding of her heart, the paralyzing feeling that made her want to turn and run back to the warm safety of the house.

If we get the check back, she thought, I'll never have to feel this kind of fear again.

If we get the check back, we can call the police. And Snowman will be gone, taken away along with the fear.

The snow had piled up against the side of the garage, some drifts up to the top of their boots. Ben reached the side door first. He hesitated and looked back, waiting for Heather to catch up.

They were both breathing hard, their breath rising in dark clouds in front of them. Heather grabbed the doorknob. It felt so cold in her bare hand, like a round icicle.

She took a deep breath and held it as she turned the knob and pushed open the door, praying that it wouldn't squeak or scrape.

The door opened silently. They stepped down the one concrete step into the dark, cluttered garage. Then they stood hand in hand, waiting for their eyes to adjust to the darkness.

Soon the outline of Aunt Belle's car became visible. Heather could make out the rake and a stack of garden tools to their left. Her uncle's power mower stood beyond that.

"Okay, this way," she whispered, giving Ben's hand a tug. His hand was as cold and clammy as hers.

The narrow stairway leading up to Snowman's room was at the back of the garage, black against the dark gray wall, as black as the opening to a cave.

"I'll go up first," Ben whispered.

"How will we find his shirt? We should have brought a flashlight," Heather whispered, shuddering.

"He'd see the light," Ben whispered. "We don't want to wake him, remember?"

Of course, Heather thought, feeling stupid.

I'm not thinking clearly. I'm in a complete panic.

She took a deep breath and let it out slowly. Then she started to follow Ben toward the blackness of the stairway.

"Oh." She bumped something with her leg, and it clattered to the garage floor.

Ben spun around.

Heather bent down to pick it up. It was a wooden broom handle. Maybe I'll hold onto this, she thought. In case Snowman wakes up. I'll have a weapon.

Had the noise alerted Snowman? They paused, listening. Nothing.

Trying to walk without making a sound, she followed Ben up the narrow, concrete steps, leaning one hand against the back wall of the garage for support as she climbed.

It seemed like an endless climb. The air felt warmer as they reached the top. The room was heated by a duct from the furnace in the basement of the house.

Snowman has all the comforts, Heather thought bitterly.

But not for long.

Ben stopped at the closed door at the top of the steps. For some reason, he turned back and looked at Heather, his features tight with fear.

"Go ahead," Heather whispered. "There's no lock."

Ben hesitated another few seconds, then turned the knob and pushed in the door. It creaked quietly as it opened.

The room was pitch-black.

Ben stepped inside, disappearing into the darkness.

Heather followed, three steps behind him.

Snowman's bed was against the back wall, under the small window. Was he sleeping in it? Heather couldn't see that far. And she couldn't hear him.

They took a few more steps into the room, walking carefully, silently over the bare floorboards. An armchair came into view a few yards in front of them. There were clothes tossed onto the chair.

They both took another step, another step, listening for the sound of Snowman's breathing.

Then the light suddenly clicked on.

"Ohh!" Heather cried out and dropped the broom handle.

"Hi, guys." Snowman was standing behind them at the doorway.

He must have heard them coming up the stairs. He must have been lying in wait for them.

Ben took a step toward him.

Snowman had an iron tire jack in his hand. He raised it high and then brought it down hard on Ben's head.

It made a horrifying *thud* as it connected.

Ben didn't make a sound as he slumped to the floor.

Then Snowman came after Heather.

Chapter 26

"Where are you taking me?"

"Shut up, Heather. Don't ask questions."

Snowman slammed down hard on the gas pedal, and Heather's car roared forward over the slick, icy road.

Heather's hands were tied behind her, the rope so tight it hurt every time she tried to move.

With Ben unconscious on the floor of his room, Snowman had grabbed her, tied her hands, then forced her out of the garage and into the house to get her bag with the car keys, covering her mouth with his gloved hand to keep her from screaming to her aunt.

Then he had shoved her roughly into the passenger seat of her car and climbed behind the wheel. Now they were speeding on North Road, past dark houses and silent, empty streets. Snowman stared straight ahead, his face calm, expressionless. Only his eyes revealed any emotion at all — and to Heather's horror, that emotion was *excitement.*

"Let me go, Snowman. I won't tell anyone about this," Heather said, not recognizing her high-pitched, frightened voice. She struggled to free her hands, but it hurt too much to move them.

Snowman stared straight ahead out the windshield. He didn't reply.

"Really, Snowman. I'll pay you. Any amount you want. Just let me go. Please."

"Shut up," he muttered under his breath.

He slammed on the brakes. The car squealed and skidded to a stop.

Heather peered out the window. The glass was entirely fogged. She couldn't see anything.

"Where are we? Snowman — please — where are we?"

He didn't answer. He climbed out and slammed his door. A few seconds later, he was pulling her roughly out of the car.

It took a few seconds for her eyes to adjust to the darkness. Then she recognized the place. Swan Park.

"Snowman — let go of me! Please. I'll pay you. I can pay you any amount. Please."

She was too frightened to think clearly. Where was he taking her? Why was he pulling her so hard?

He dragged her up the sloping, snow-covered hill, then toward the woods.

"Snowman, please — "

"Our favorite spot," he said quietly, calmly.

He pulled her faster, both hands around her arm. She couldn't resist. If she tried to pull back, the rope around her hands cut into her wrists.

"Our secret spot," he said, a strange smile on his face. "Our own secret spot. No one will find you here, Heather. No one can interrupt us now."

He pulled her to the circular clearing in the woods, the clearing where they had built their snowman. There was no sign of the snowman now. The small, hidden clearing was filled with fresh snow.

It's so dark. And so still. So unreal, Heather thought.

What's he going to do to me now?

"Let me go," she said, giving it one last try. "I'll give you all the money I have. I promise. And I won't tell anyone about . . . anything. Please, Snowman!"

He turned to her, that same strange smile on his face. "Heather, you're such a bad little liar."

He moved closer, lowering his head.

He's going to kiss me, she thought.

But then she felt a stab of pain, blinding, throbbing pain, on the back of her head.

And everything faded to black.

Chapter 27

Heather opened her eyes, but everything remained black.

I'm blind, she thought.

The back of her head throbbed with pain. He hit me over the head, and now I'm blind.

No.

She tried to move. Couldn't.

I'm not blind. I'm inside something. I'm wrapped inside something.

She tried to move her hands, but the shock of pain made her stop. They were still tied. Her feet were tied, too, she realized.

Where am I?

It was hard to breathe. The air was cold but stale.

I'm not blind. I'm not blind. I'm not blind.

And I haven't gone crazy.

He's wrapped me in something hard and cold. And I can't move, can't break out.

She heard a scraping sound from somewhere outside the shell she was in. She could feel tapping and pounding on her back.

A familiar thudding sound.

The sound of snow being packed.

It was so cold, so dark in here.

And suddenly she realized where she was.

I'm packed in snow.

He's packed me in snow. I'm *inside* a snowman. He's crazy. He's truly crazy.

Who would think of such a thing? It's impossible! Impossible, but Heather knew it was true.

She could feel Snowman putting on the finishing touches, packing the snow more tightly around her.

I'm a living mummy. A living snow mummy.

But not for long. Soon the air will be gone. Soon I'll be a *dead* snow mummy.

And no one will find me.

No one will look in this clearing. No one knows about this clearing.

And no one could see me anyway—until the snow melts.

No one will find my body until the snow melts.

My frozen body.

No!

She had to move, had to push her way out.

She tried leaning forward. Maybe she could fall forward, fall out of it.

No. It was packed too tightly. She couldn't move at all.

Snowman seemed to have left. She couldn't hear him. She couldn't feel him packing on more snow.

I've got to get my hands free, she thought. I've got to ignore the pain and get my hands free. Then maybe I can push my way out.

She tried twisting her wrists. It hurt so much. The rope was wet now, and it cut even more painfully.

Think, Heather. Try to think clearly. What can you do? What can you do to free yourself?

She took a deep breath, inhaling the stale, frozen air, and fought the panic back.

She listened. Was he still there?

Was he standing there admiring his snowman, his living snowman?

Or had he driven away in her car, left her there to suffocate and freeze?

No. I won't die here. I won't die inside this thing.

Ignoring the searing pain, she twisted her wrists from side to side.

"Ohhh."

It was so cold. So dark and so cold.

To her surprise, the rope seemed to give a little.

"Ow!"

She twisted the wrist a little harder, a little faster.

Yes. The rope was definitely slipping.

Yes. She was loosening it. Yes. She could feel it move.

A few seconds later, her right hand was free. She moved the fingers, trying to exercise the numbness from them.

Then she tried to raise her arm.

No room. She couldn't move it.

The snow was packed so tightly, she couldn't raise it.

Then she remembered the lighter in her jeans pocket, the butane lighter she always carried.

Could she reach it?

If so, maybe she could burn her way out of the snowman. Or at least melt enough snow to be able to push through it.

There was so little room to move in.

It was so cold, so dark.

But she didn't care about that now. She was close to getting out. She knew that. With just a little more effort, with just the *right* effort, she could get out.

I *will* get out, she told herself.

And yes — her hand was in her jeans pocket.

And yes — it gripped the butane lighter.

And yes — she managed to pull it out of the pocket.

And raised it just a little. And pointed the head of the lighter away from her and toward the snow.

"No!"

She almost dropped it.

Gripping it more tightly, she fumbled it toward the snow again. And moved her finger up to the top.

She closed her eyes, even though she couldn't see anything anyway, and hoping, hoping against hope, hoping with all her strength, flicked the lighter.

It didn't work.

Chapter 28

"Oh, please. Please light."

She hadn't tried the lighter in years. It was probably completely dry.

As dry as her hopes.

As dead as her future.

Gasping in the stale air of her frozen prison, she flicked the lighter again.

Please, please — light!

No.

It didn't work.

About to give up, she flicked it one more time.

This time it flamed.

She saw the flaring light, then felt the heat of it.

She held it against the snow till it burned through, leaving a small hole. Then she raised it a bit, and the hole enlarged.

When it was big enough, she clicked off the lighter, gripping it tightly in her fist, raised her arm, and pushed her fist through the snow.

Yes!

One side of the snowman crumbled away.

She frantically pushed snow out of the way, breathing deeply, uttering low cries of happiness, of relief.

I'm out! I'm free!

I did it!

Now to untie my feet.

"Oh! You!"

She wasn't free yet.

Snowman stood watching her, his dark eyes cold and calm, his hands in his overcoat pockets.

She wanted to cry out, scream at him. But her breath caught in her throat.

He shook his head.

"Looks like I have to kill you the hard way," he said, his voice soft, nonchalant.

He pulled off the long red wool scarf he was wearing around his neck and, stretching it taut between his hands, moved toward her quickly.

Chapter 29

"No!"

Heather tried to move away, but her feet were tightly tied, and she fell face forward into the snow.

He grabbed her and pulled her up.

His eyes as cold and smooth as black marbles, he raised the scarf and started to wrap it around her neck.

"No!"

She didn't even think about the lighter, didn't think about what she was doing.

She flicked the top and the flame shot out, a streak of orange against the blackness of the night.

Snowman's face filled with confusion. Then he screamed in fright as the front of his old overcoat burst into flames.

"Hey — *help!*"

He's actually lost his cool, she thought.

And her next thought: What have I done?

She stood as if paralyzed as he slapped at the flaming overcoat with both gloved hands.

But the coat was ablaze. He looked like a frantic, wriggling torch.

"Help me!"

He tried pulling off the coat. But he couldn't unbutton it with his gloves on.

Screaming in pain and fear, he dived into the snow, rolling quickly.

His screams echoed off the trees.

The flames started to diminish. But his screams seemed to grow louder.

No. It was another sound she was hearing. A sound far off on the other side of the trees.

A wailing sound. Growing louder, louder.

"Help me!"

The flashing red lights roared right through the woods and squealed to a halt at the edge of the clearing.

There were two sets of lights, flashing red against the darkness.

It took Heather a while to realize that they were police cars.

It all seemed to be happening so fast, too fast to grasp it all, too fast to believe it.

But there were police officers jumping out of the two cars. Two of them were huddled over Snowman, who was lying still, so still on his stomach in the snow.

Two others came running over to Heather.

"Are you all right?" one of them asked, his face flashing red then black, red then black.

"Yeah, I guess."

And then there was Ben, a large cross-shaped bandage on top of his black hair. He ran quickly over the snow to her side, looking very concerned, bending down to untie her feet, then putting his arm comfortingly around her shoulders.

"Hey — this is the kid the FBI is looking for," one of the police officers near Snowman exclaimed.

"Radio for an ambulance. He's burned pretty bad."

"Ben — " Heather said, struggling to clear her head, struggling to make sense of everything.

"You're okay," he said soothingly. "Just relax. You're okay. Everything's going to be okay now."

"But — how did you know, Ben? How did you know where to find me?"

She turned and stared at him, as if searching for the answer in his eyes. He looked away, embarrassed.

"That day," he said finally. "That day you and Snowman came here and built that snowman?"

"Yes?"

"Well . . . I was so jealous, Heather. I guess I was a little out of my head or something. I . . . uh . . . I followed you. I watched you. From those trees over there."

"I saw you!" Heather exclaimed. "I *knew* I saw someone spying on us."

"Yeah, that was me," Ben said guiltily.

"I'm so glad!" Heather cried, and threw her arms around him, hugging him tightly.

"I just acted on a hunch tonight," Ben explained. "This was such a hidden, secluded place. I just guessed he might take you here. Lucky guess, huh?"

"Yeah. Lucky guess." Heather smiled for the first time in a long while, her arms still around Ben's shoulders.

But her smile quickly faded. "The check," she said. "Snowman must have the check in his shirt pocket."

They hurried over to where Snowman was lying, unconscious. The police officers had carefully rolled him onto his back. The entire front of his overcoat was burned away, the material tattered and blackened. The front of his shirt was also burned completely away.

The check had burned up with it.

"He'll be okay. The burns look like they're all superficial," one of the police officers told Heather.

"Can I go home now?" Heather asked.

"I guess. I can see you've had a rough night. Your boyfriend there has already told us some of it on the way over here, but I'll need to get your story first thing in the morning."

Heather agreed and, suddenly feeling exhausted, started toward the car, Ben gently guiding her, his arm around her waist. Suddenly she turned back and looked at the clearing, at the shattered clumps of hard snow that had been her snowman prison.

"It's okay," Ben said.

"I hated my uncle!" Heather declared. "If I hadn't let myself hate him so much . . ."

"You can't blame yourself," Ben said.

She turned back to Ben. "It's like I was frozen with hate. But not anymore. Not ever again."

Ben pulled her close. "You *are* getting warmer," he said.

This was one time she *didn't* laugh at one of Ben's jokes. Instead, she groaned and gave him a hard but playful shove. Then, leaning against each other, they made their way over the smooth, pale snow to her car.

About the Author

R. L. STINE is the author of more than seventy
books of humor, adventure, and mystery for young
readers. He has written more than a dozen scary
thrillers such as this one.

He lives in New York City with his wife, Jane,
and their son, Matt.

MYSTERY THRILLERS

Introducing a new series of hard-hitting action-packed thrillers for young adults.

THE SONG OF THE DEAD by Anthony Masters
For the first time in years "the song of the dead" is heard around Whitstable. Is it really the cries of dead sailors? Or is it something more sinister? Barney Hampton is determined to get to the bottom of the mystery . . .

THE FERRYMAN'S SON by Ian Strachan
Rob is convinced that Drewe and Miles are up to no good. Where do they go on their night cruises? And why does Kimberley go with them? When Kimberley disappears Rob finds himself embroiled in a web of deadly intrigue . . .

TREASURE OF GREY MANOR by Terry Deary
When Jamie Williams and Trish Grey join forces for a school history project, they unearth much more than they bargain for! The diary of the long-dead Marie Grey hints at the existence of hidden treasure. But Jamie and Trish aren't the only ones interested in the treasure – and some people don't mind playing dirty . . .

THE FOGGIEST by Dave Belbin
As Rachel and Matt Gunn move into their new home, a strange fog descends over the country. Then Rachel and Matt's father disappears from his job at the weather station, and they discover the sinister truth behind the fog . . .

BLUE MURDER by Jay Kelso
One foggy night Mack McBride is walking along the pier when he hears a scream and a splash. Convinced that a murder has been committed he decides to investigate and finds himself in more trouble than he ever dreamed of . . .

DEAD MAN'S SECRET by Linda Allen
After Annabel's Uncle Nick is killed in a rock-climbing accident, she becomes caught up in a nerve-wracking chain of events. Helped by her friends Simon and Julie, she discovers Uncle Nick was involved in some very unscrupulous activities . . .

CROSSFIRE by Peter Beere
After running away from Southern Ireland Maggie finds herself roaming the streets of London destitute and alone. To make matters worse, her step-father is an important member of the IRA – if he doesn't find her before his enemies do, she might just find herself caught up in the crossfire . . .

THE THIRD DRAGON by Garry Kilworth
Following the massacre at Tiananmen Square Xu flees to Hong Kong, where he is befriended by John Tenniel, and his two friends Peter and Jenny. They hide him in a hillside cave, but soon find themselves swept up in a hazardous adventure that could have deadly results . . .

VANISHING POINT by Anthony Masters
In a strange dream, Danny sees his father's train vanishing into a tunnel, never to be seen again. When Danny's father really does disappear, Danny and his friend Laura are drawn into a criminal world, far more deadly than they could ever have imagined . . .